C000133654

CLOSER TO YOU

ADAM CROFT

Enjoy the book,
Angela!

BLACK CANNON
PUBLISHING

First published in Great Britain in 2020.

This edition published in 2021 by Black Cannon Publishing.

ISBN: 978-1-912599-70-7

A CIP catalogue record for this book is available from the British Library.

Printed and bound in Great Britain by Clays Ltd, Elcograf S.p.A.

MORE BOOKS BY ADAM CROFT

RUTLAND CRIME SERIES

1. What Lies Beneath
2. On Borrowed Time
3. In Cold Blood

KNIGHT & CULVERHOUSE CRIME THRILLERS

1. Too Close for Comfort
2. Guilty as Sin
3. Jack Be Nimble
4. Rough Justice
5. In Too Deep
6. In The Name of the Father
7. With A Vengeance
8. Dead & Buried
9. In Too Deep
10. Snakes & Ladders

PSYCHOLOGICAL THRILLERS

- Her Last Tomorrow

- Only The Truth
- In Her Image
- Tell Me I'm Wrong
- The Perfect Lie
- Closer To You

KEMPSTON HARDWICK MYSTERIES

1. Exit Stage Left
2. The Westerlea House Mystery
3. Death Under the Sun
4. The Thirteenth Room
5. The Wrong Man

All titles are available to order from all good book shops.

Signed and personalised books available at adamcroft.net/shop

EBOOK-ONLY SHORT STORIES

- Gone
- The Harder They Fall
- Love You To Death
- The Defender

To find out more, visit adamcroft.net

PROLOGUE

I always knew you'd be out there somewhere. They say there's someone for everyone. And I've found you. Again.

A needle in the haystack, a shining diamond amongst the dirt. And there's plenty of dirt out there, believe me. You wouldn't believe the amount of dross I've had to wade through to find you. These days the world seems to be filled with trout pouts and Snapchat filters. But I knew you wouldn't care for any of that. It's just not you.

It's been a long time coming. You don't know how much I've gone through to find you. The sacrifices I've made. If only you knew. One day, you will.

It was always meant to be this way. Sooner or later you'll realise that. There were times where I could have given up, could have thought it would never happen. But I didn't. And then I saw you.

That first photo was enough. The smile. Those eyes. Your face shape was ideal. But that wasn't what I noticed first.

I don't know how long I held my breath for. I think I thought I was dreaming. I recognised it immediately. It transported me back, made me smile, made me happy. You made me happy. It almost seemed too good to be true, but I knew that wasn't possible. You were always true. You were always there.

In that moment, I knew I had to have you. I knew it was you. It was perfect. Almost too perfect.

1

The whole 'dating' scene isn't something I ever thought I'd be involved with.

There's a part of me which thinks dating apps are somewhat crude and soulless. After all, all you see is a name, age and a photo and you're asking to swipe right, indicating you'd totally marry this guy based on those three things or swipe left, consigning him to oblivion as not even worth speaking to because he's six months too old or dared to wear sunglasses while having his photo taken.

Another part of me realises that's the way things have been done for years, anyway. If you spot someone in a bar or pub you know nothing about them. Even less than you do on these apps, in fact. At least with the app you know their name and age before you talk to them. And who wants to date a Kevin?

Maybe I've just been out of the game too long. It's definitely easier than going out to meet people, and means I can at least vet them before having to come face to face with them. That's something I've been grateful for on more than one occasion recently.

I've been using Tinder for about three weeks now. I've not met up with anyone from it, but I will. There've been plenty who've managed to rule themselves out of the running, though. Guys who open with cheesy chat-up lines get unmatched immediately. Anyone who mentions sex inside the first three messages meets a similar fate.

I'm talking to two at the moment. Finn is 32. He calls himself an 'Irish stallion', but the conversation is dull. I didn't realise he'd be as scintillating to talk to as an actual horse. Ryan is 29, apparently, although I'd put him north of 35. The age thing doesn't bother me, but the lying does. Still, he reckons he's 29 and I'm not about to ask for his birth certificate. In any case, he's started to get sleazy and ask about my bedroom preferences, so he won't last much longer.

I decide to go back to the main screen on the app and see who else is about. The first few are definite left swipes. Topless photos are always a no-no, as are people called Gary. But I swipe right on a couple, too. I've got a thing for nice eyes. I think you can tell a lot by looking into someone's eyes. I guess there's a reason they call them the windows to the soul. There are some guys who have those 'serial killer eyes' that you can't quite explain, but which everyone recognises. And others have a cheeky little glint, almost as if the niceness is trying to push through.

Tom's eyes are warm, inviting. And there's a definite cheeky glint. I swipe right on him, and a new screen pops up telling me it's a match. Tom had already swiped right on me in the past. That means we're now able to talk to each other.

I think about what to say to him. I'm not good with openers. I don't want to go down the boring 'Hi' route, but what else is there to say to someone you don't know but are expected to speak to? This is why us women tend to let guys make the first move. They seem to know what to do. Well, some of them do.

I have a closer look at his profile for some inspiration. Maybe there's something on there I can lead in with. It doesn't say much, though.

Positive, open-minded and friendly. Still seeking the yin to my yang. I know she can't be far off. Maybe it's you?

Perhaps a little cheesy and unoriginal, but there's something I like about that. He doesn't come across as trying to be something he's not, unlike 90% of the guys on Tinder who claim to be surfing vegan martial artists who visit sixty countries a year and go to the gym every three hours. If that was the case, local leisure centres and the departures lounge at Luton Airport would be reclassified as zoo exhibits for the male of the species.

While I'm still thinking of what to say to Tom, a message pops up on the screen. He got there first. That's no bad thing, and at least it shows he has some confidence in making the first move.

Hi Grace! Gorgeous photos, especially the one with the butterfly dress. It's an Apricot one, isn't it? x

I feel my eyebrows flick upwards, momentarily and voluntarily. This guy knows what he's doing.

I'm impressed. So which are you, fashion designer or drag artist? x

He's keen. I see the three dots appear on the screen almost immediately, which tells me he's already composing a reply. After a few seconds, it appears.

Haha - neither I'm afraid. I was a friend of mine's 'shopping buddy' for a while and I think I've probably memorised every dress in that shop x

I have a little chuckle at the thought of him being dragged around shopping centres, laden with bags while his friend tries on every dress in sight.

Always on the lookout for a bag carrier. So is it a good thing or a bad thing that I reminded you of your friend? :P x

Can't go wrong with a cheeky little tongue-sticky-out face. At least it shows I'm only teasing.

She's got a boyfriend now so I've been relieved of my duties. And relieved is definitely the right word! You remind me of lots of things, but I'm not about to wheel those old lines out. I'd put you off your breakfast. Much planned for the day? x

Just work, I type. I'm not sure whether that's preferable to listening to cheesy chat-up lines or not. It's a tough one... What do you do for a living? x

I lock my phone for a moment or two and make another cup of tea. Glancing at the clock, I reckon I've got plenty of time for another before I have to leave and catch my train.

While the kettle's on, I decide to do a bit of washing up. The little boiler on the wall creaks and groans like a teenager I've just woken up and asked to warm the water by hand. Still, I can't complain. The cost of this place is actually pretty good for this part of the south east. Even though I'm just outside of London, not too far down the road they're renting out cupboards for two grand a month. It's still far from being manageable on my own, though.

Since Matt and I split up, my parents have been covering his half of the mortgage. They didn't need to, but they've always been incredibly supportive. They know I couldn't get anywhere else near work for the same sort of money. Not in a million years. If I moved further north I'd spend my life commuting and would spend any money I'd saved on travel. Besides which, this is my home. I've always lived in the area, and I've become attached to my little house. Sure, I could take on a lodger or a housemate, but they'd be a complete stranger. Everyone I know is part-nered off and has their own place.

This place was ours. Mine and Matt's. Well, it was always mine on paper. His credit score was so shot to pieces, and his income so low, it was actually better not to have his name on the mortgage. But it doesn't feel right moving a stranger in, even after what he did. Besides which, it's a tiny one-bedroom house and I can't ask someone to pay half the mortgage and then pop them on a camp bed in the living room.

I pour my cup of tea and check my phone. There's another message on Tinder from Tom.

I'm a sales manager for a tech security firm. We provide computer security gear for companies all over the world. All pretty boring, but good fun x

I think that's the first and last time I'll see the words 'computer security gear' and 'good fun' in the same paragraph.

Nice! Does that involve lots of travel? x

As soon as I send the reply I start to question myself.

Will he think I'm trying to work out whether he'll be around much? I don't want to sound as if I'm already sussing him out for long-term relationship potential. Before I can worry too much, the reply comes in.

Some, but nothing too heavy. What do you do? x

In a way, I'm glad Tom didn't tell me he was a fireman or a brain surgeon, because I always struggle to make my job sound interesting. I love it, though, and I guess that's the main thing.

I work in events management. Again, pretty boring but good fun ;) x

I don't know what made me wheel out the winking face emoji, but it felt right. Again, I worry that he'll get the wrong end of the stick and associate it with the 'good fun' comment. Oh well. If he starts to get randy I'll kick him into touch with the others.

Sounds interesting! By the way, if you want to move to WhatsApp or something at any point, I'm on 07700 900624. Tinder can be a bit unreliable with messages some-times! No pressure though x

I smile at this. He's not the first person to suggest swap-ping numbers fairly early on, but he's got a good point. The app does have a habit of crashing or losing access to messages. And anyway, he seems alright. I save the number in my phone as a backup but decide to stick to Tinder for now.

Thanks - will save for future reference ;) Anyway, better dash now. Long day ahead. Chat later? x

The reply comes within a few seconds.

Definitely. Looking forward to it already xx

2

I love my job, but it definitely has its stressful moments. Today has been full of them. I've been working on a launch event for a new art gallery in town — the sort of thing which should be fairly straightforward. Unfortunately for me, the client loves changing her mind every five minutes, which makes the whole exercise a thousand times more tedious than it needs to be.

At one point, she even wanted to change the location of the event. The official opening of an art gallery, held somewhere that isn't the art gallery. How do you square that one? Thankfully, I managed to talk her out of it, but that came at the expense of having to give in to other, almost equally ridiculous, demands.

She was determined she wanted some form of celebrity to do the opening, but there was nothing else attached to that particular instruction. She claimed to know plenty of celebrities, but they'd all be attending as friends and couldn't possibly be the ones to cut the ribbon. She didn't tell me if she wanted a musician, actor, politician, artist, reality show star, sportsperson or what constituted a suitable level of celebrity for her precious gallery.

In the end I phoned up a couple of agents I knew, asking if they had anyone in town on that date who might be willing to turn up for a couple of hours for a reasonable fee and some bubbly. Ultimately, we settled on a TV personality who presents a daytime antiques programme and was willing to take five hundred quid for popping in to cut the ribbon.

It infuriates me to have to do it, but we need to try and keep her sweet. Work's been slow for us this year, particularly after a rival company set up in the area.

Pelham-Saunders has been trying to aim itself at the same high-end clients as we've traditionally chased, and for some reason they've been winning them. We've been losing pitches to them left, right and centre, and there've been rumours that we might have to let some people go. I'm fortunate enough to be well-liked by the bosses, and the buzz in the office is always positive and friendly, so I'm pretty sure we can pull through it. We've got through worse.

I'm working on updating the budget spreadsheet and trying to figure out where we might be able to lose a zero so I don't have to make that awkward call to her to let her know she's going to need to lower her demands or increase her budget. Just as I'm doing so, an email alert pops up on my computer screen.

It's from her.

I sigh inwardly, my heart dropping a little as I know exactly what sort of thing it will be. She's either changed her mind about the celebrity, had a brilliant idea to make the party dragon-themed or has decided to turn the art gallery into a shoe shop.

I open the email and read what it says. All of a sudden, my previous thoughts don't seem all that funny or outrageous anymore.

Hi Grace,

I've been having another think about the launch event and I think we might be going down the wrong road with the colour theme.

I was reading an article in Cosmo which talked about the implications of colours and the psychological effects they can induce. I know we talked about purple being quite a regal and upmarket colour, but the article said it's also seen as pompous and conveys emotions of loneliness and desperation — NOT things we want to be associated with, as I'm sure you agree!

I think instead we should go for classy neutrals, with a base colour of white. Apparently that is pure, clean and conveys

*brightness of spirit. Definitely the sort of feelings we want to
communicate.*

*I trust all is in hand and you'll be able to make the necessary
changes.*

*Yours,
Matilda*

I can feel the blood rising in my face as I read the email
again, sure I must have misunderstood. We've got a week
left until the event. One week. And she wants to change the
bloody colour scheme?

I go to compose a reply, but decide against it. If I send
something back to her now, we'll end up losing the contract.
No doubt about that. Over the years I've become pretty
good at biting my tongue, but every now and again I need to
take some space.

In any case, there's not long to go now until Christmas.
The office shuts down completely over the festive period
and everyone goes pretty much incommunicado, with Sue,
the director, having decreed a couple of years earlier that
email access should be banned over the break. It's a modern
approach, but one which is definitely appreciated.

I stand up from my desk, grab my bag and head for the
loos. I need to calm down.

When I get there, I dump my bag on the side, lean back
against the cold tiled wall and exhale. I take my phone out

of my bag and look at the screen. There's a Tinder message
from Tom, sent an hour or so earlier.

Hope you're having a good day. Speak soon x

I smile, realising that he's been thinking of me, even
though his day has doubtless been as busy as mine. I'd be
lying if I said I'd spent the morning thinking about him, but
I have a funny feeling the afternoon might be different.

I unlock my phone and tap out a reply.

*Not brilliant, to be honest. But I guess that's what makes the
evenings all the sweeter x*

Within a minute or so, he's sent me another message.

Oh no. Hope all's OK...? x

Yeah, all fine, I reply. *Just the usual work stuff! Hope your
day is going better x*

I don't like to jump the gun, but he's doing all the right
things. He's kind, attentive, communicative — all without
being creepy or going overboard.

I take the opportunity to touch up my makeup. I don't
wear a lot, but the act of applying it somehow tends to make
me feel better.

As I do so, I hear my phone buzz.

Would it make you feel better if you had something to look forward to? x

I think I know what he's getting at, but I decide to play dumb.

Such as? x

His reply comes barely ten seconds later.

Would you like to grab a drink somewhere tonight? x

I look at the words on the screen in front of me, unsure how to reply. Would I like to? Yes. Obviously. Do I think I should? I'm less sure. I'm not in the habit of meeting people I've only been speaking to on an app for a couple of days, but at the same time he does seem like a genuinely nice person. And anyway, what harm can come of a quick drink in a local — public — bar? I'm in no more danger than I would be if I just happened to bump into him while out. He's an actual person, after all. I'm not some sort of super-natural proxy which is going to enable his crossing over from The Internet to The Real World.

Why the hell not, I tell myself. I've had enough of the mundanity of the day — the week — and he's right: it will give me something to look forward to. What harm has a little spontaneity ever done anyone?

Sure. Where were you thinking? x

As far as I'm concerned, this is the real test of a man. I like someone who can take control, make decisions. If he comes back asking me where *I'd* like to go, he loses a point. If he makes a suggestion or takes some sort of positive action, it's game on.

His reply arrives.

Brownlow Arms, 8pm? x

A place and a time. And it's local to me — to both of us, I assume. His Tinder profile said we were 4km away from each other. At least I can be pretty sure there won't be two Brownlow Armses around there.

Perfect. See you then x

I smile. I can already feel my day getting better.

3

The Brownlow Arms used to be a dark and dingy country pub, but it's recently been spruced up to become a light and airy gastropub. It's not exactly in the country, either, rather nestled in a small hamlet between two smallish towns. It's the sort of place that'd never survive if it didn't do food, which I guess is one of the saving graces of the rise of the gastropub.

Tom messaged me again in the afternoon to let me know one half of the pub was for dining only, so he'd meet me in the bar area and we could find a drinks-only table from there.

I get there just over ten minutes early, having called a cab from my house. I definitely need a drink after the day I've had. I'm not the sort of person who likes to be late, and I prefer to get my bearings and feel comfortable with my surroundings before things kick off. I've not been in here since they've done it up. In fact, I don't think I ever came in here before they did it up. It's busy for a weekday evening, and I wonder how many of the couples and families will be heading through to the restaurant to eat.

I order a soft drink from the bar — don't want to be getting too far ahead of myself — and sit down at a small table in the corner by the window. At least this way I'll be able to see when Tom arrives. He'll be driving, he said, as he needs to be up early for work in the morning.

After a few minutes, I see a white Audi pull into the car park. PCP White, my dad would call it, referring to the fact that so many people decided to 'buy' cars on Personal Contract Purchase plans nowadays, and kept the monthly payments down by choosing the basic white paintwork. I watch as Tom gets out of the car, and I decide I probably won't tell him that little anecdote.

He's instantly recognisable from his picture, and that immediately earns him an extra point. Too many people seem to have old photos on their profile, or ones which have been doctored or filtered to make them look better than they actually do. He's taller than I imagined, but not by much. He's wearing a smart jumper over a shirt with light-coloured chinos and brown shoes, and seems as though he'd fit in perfectly with the rest of the clientele here. Might have to be careful I don't lose him in a crowd.

He spots me as soon as he walks in, and I stand up as he makes his way over and plants a kiss on my cheek.

'How are you?' he asks.

'I'm good,' I reply. 'Busy in here tonight.'

'Must have chosen the right place then,' he says, winking. 'Would you like a drink?'

I've nearly finished my soft drink, so I tell him I'd like a glass of red. I stare absentmindedly out the window until he comes back from the bar with a non-alcoholic beer, and he sits down on the opposite side of the table.

'So whereabouts do you live?' he says. 'I don't think we ever actually did that bit.'

I laugh and tell him I live in the next town along. He lives in the opposite direction, but only a couple of miles away. I go to say it's odd we've never bumped into each other before, but I'm not originally from round here and, judging by his accent, neither is he.

'Cornwall,' he says when I ask him about it. 'Decided to stop crunching carrots and upped sticks to head here.'

His accent is more rounded than the typical West Country burr, so I ask him how long he's been up here.

'Not long,' he says. 'Personally I'd love to lose the accent completely. Not exactly got good memories of the place.'

I want to find out more, but can't exactly ask him to explain what he means. I decide to try another way around it.

'Not keen to head back, then?'

He lets out a sarcastic chuckle and shakes his head. 'No I am not. It's a bit of a long story, but I might as well be open and honest from the start. I was married. We had a daughter. I totally understand if you want to get up and run now. Most do.'

'Seriously? Why would they do that?'

Tom shrugs. 'Dunno. I guess they have these ideas about how they'd like things to be. My baggage doesn't quite fit into those plans.'

'What happened?' I ask. 'I mean, you don't have to tell me if you don't want to. I'm just genuinely interested.'

Tom lets out a deep breath. 'Well, all seemed to be going fine. One day I came home and found a note on the kitchen table saying she wanted a fresh start and they were gone. That was the last I heard from her.'

'Jesus. And she still lives down there?'

'So I'm told. But her family won't tell me a thing, obviously. Looking back, she was always going to self-destruct.'

'So when was all this?' I ask, trying to work out the dates in my mind.

'A couple of years ago now. Seems like an age.'

'So you don't see your daughter?'

'No,' he says quietly, his face dropping. 'I shelled out thousands trying to track her down. Hired a private detective, the lot. But she made up a load of stories about me so I couldn't get joint custody. I almost lost my job. I worked from home most of the time, and obviously after all this I didn't have a home. I couldn't afford to keep the house by myself. I travel quite a bit for work anyway, so I knew it'd be handy to be closer to London and the airports and to give me a fresh start. My boss put me up in a flat he owns up

here. This was all a little while after, of course. I stayed
down in Cornwall for a long time, hoping things might
work out. But after a year and a half or so, I was out of
money and couldn't keep the house on. I've been up here
for three or four months now.'

I wasn't expecting this. I wasn't expecting any of this.
'Wow,' I say. 'Sorry to hear that.'

'The car's not mine either,' he says, somehow managing
to get there before me. 'That's my boss's too. He gets a
company car, so he uses that and lets me use the Audi.'

'Wow. Sounds like a good friend.'

'He is, yeah. I'd be lost without him. He's kept me on
my feet.'

'What about your family? Do you still have them?'

'No,' Tom says, his face dropping slightly. 'My parents
died.'

'I'm sorry,' I say. 'Was it recent?'

'Fairly. A couple of years back. Car accident. Sorry, you
must think I'm some sort of mental case.'

'No, not at all,' I say, reaching across the table and
putting my hand on his forearm. 'We've all been through
things. It doesn't make you a worse person. It just makes
you human.'

We chat for another two hours, mostly about nothing
but enough to let me find out more about him. I come to
admire his positive outlook. Even after everything he's been
through, after almost losing everything, he still manages to
hold a smile and look to the future. There were one or two

negative comments, of course, but on the whole he seemed to be determined to make his life better in every way he could. I can't speak for anyone else, but I always find that to be attractive in a man.

With the time past ten o'clock, we make our way out into the car park, where my taxi's waiting. Tom offered me a lift, but I insisted he didn't need to go out of his way. In any case, I wasn't quite comfortable with him knowing where I live just yet — not that I told him that. A true gentleman, he didn't push the point and insisted instead that he pay for the taxi.

As we say our goodbyes, I lean in and kiss him.

Later that night, while I'm getting ready for bed, I see another message pop up on my phone. It's him.

I hope I'm not jumping the gun here, but I really like you. I think you might be the ying to my yang x

I smile, and tap out a reply.

4

Today was much more bearable than yesterday, largely because I had Tom's messages to keep me going — as well as memories of our second date from last night.

We met up for a bite to eat, then went bowling in town. It's not my usual cup of tea, but Tom suggested it and I thought at least we'd be able to chat and get to know each other, rather than sitting in silence in a cinema somewhere.

It's not like me to be out two nights in a row, but I'd already arranged to go round to Cath's this evening to help her with her wedding plans.

Cath and Ben have been together for almost five years, and announced last year that they'd got engaged. I don't think they quite realised how much work would go into planning a wedding, though, and I've ended up being appointed their unofficial wedding organiser. I don't mind that one bit, though. I'm quite enjoying it, and looking forward to making sure they both have their best day of their lives. Cath being Cath, she decided they'd get married on Valentine's Day, because she thought it would be romantic.

'The main thing now is to sort out the seating plan,' I tell her, as we sit down in her living room with a glass of wine. 'Is Ben around? He should probably be in on this.'

'I sent him to the pub,' Cath tells me. 'We tried to sort it out ourselves, but we just keep disagreeing. He's got this bee in his bonnet that the numbers need to be even on both sides. Well, his mum has, anyway. Problem is, I've got a huge family. He's an only child and so were both of his parents, but there's four of us on my side, plus twelve cousins. If there's going to be even numbers on both sides, his mum'll end up inviting her second cousin three times removed before my brother's even got a seat.'

We sit down on her living room floor and move pieces of paper around for a good half an hour before realising there's no fair or democratic way to do it. The numbers are going to be unbalanced in any case.

'You've either got to stop at cousins, or whatever line on the family tree you choose, or match numbers on both sides. You can't do both,' I tell her.

'I know. I've been telling Ben that for months. His mum's still under the impression we're going to invite more people from her side of the family. He's going to have to say something to her pretty quickly. We can't go inviting people at this stage, not so long after all the invitations have gone out. They'll know they're afterthoughts.'

In the end, we decide to go for a plan that couldn't possibly upset anybody: complete randomness. We write all the couples' names on pieces of paper — as well as anyone attending on their own — and put them in a bowl. Then we mix them up and take them out one by one, seating them around our imaginary tables. They get what they're given.

'Ah. Problem,' Cath says, scrunching up her face. 'Uncle Mike can't sit there.'

'Why not?' I ask.

'He used to be married to Teri. Can't have them on the same table.'

'So move him back a couple of tables.'

'But he's my dad's brother. We can't really have him at the back.'

'We're going for randomness, Cath. No hierarchy, remember?'

'Even so. There must be somewhere else we can put him.'

I sigh. 'Well let's move Teri instead. Mike can stay where he is, near the front.'

'But she's my mum's best friend. And she needs to be on that table, because it's closest to the disabled toilet.'

I'm starting to see why wedding planning tends to cause so many rifts and arguments in families.

'I tell you what,' I say. 'I went to one last year which was ridiculously informal. They had a chip van outside the venue that did the catering. Everyone queued up for their fish and chips, then went and sat down wherever the hell they wanted. People moved about, got up and mingled, it was great. Why not do that? You can still save a seat near the disabled toilet for Teri, and as far as her and Uncle Mike are concerned, never the twain shall meet.'

Cath scrunches up her face. 'A chip van?'

'Obviously I'm not suggesting that bit, but scrapping the seating plan would solve your problems.'

'What about the food, though? The venue need a list of everyone who needs the vegetarian or gluten free options. They'd be running around like blue-arsed flies trying to find the right people if we did that.'

'Some sort of table marker then,' I suggest. 'Like when you go to a pub and you take a wooden spoon with a number on it. Maybe have colour coded ones, so people who've ordered the vegetarian or gluten free options can make themselves known.'

Cath's got that look on her face which tells me she can't see any flaws in my logic, but still doesn't like the idea because it's not quite how she envisioned it. I take the opportunity to move onto the next item on the list — preparing the wedding favours.

As we make them, I bring up the subject of Tom. Everything happened so fast yesterday, I haven't had a chance to update her yet.

'Tinder strikes again, eh?' she says.

'Honestly, he's really nice. You'll like him.'

Cath smiles. 'Good,' she says. 'You know, there's still time to put him down as your plus one for the wedding. If he gets his meal choice in within the next few weeks, he can come to the day too.'

'Oh, I think that's a bit soon,' I say. 'I only met him a week ago.'

'I know,' Cath says, smiling again. 'Just saying. You deserve someone. Especially after what happened.'

I don't think it was necessary for her to bring up Matt, but it's too late now. The damage is done.

'Yeah. Well, let's look to the future, shall we?' I say.

'Of course. What's he like?'

'Tom? He seems really nice. Very open and honest. He told me all about himself, which I liked. Clearly got nothing to hide. He's gorgeous too, obviously.'

'Obviously,' Cath says, giggling.

'He's a proper gentleman, too. Polite, respectful. He even offered to pick me up and drop me off home from yours later, so I didn't have to walk back in the dark.'

'Blimey. What did you say?'

'Well, I didn't want to sound ungrateful, so I told him that was lovely of him to offer and I'd see how things went and let him know. Didn't want to commit, but didn't want to seem like a bitch either.'

Cath shrugs. 'Then say yes. It's hardly commitment to

cadge a lift home, is it? And anyway, it gives me a chance to meet him.'

I smile. Cath's always had good instincts. She's rarely wrong about things. I take her at her word, and I send Tom a message to see if the offer of a lift is still on.

We spend the next hour and a half trying to finesse the table plan, before I accept Cath was right: it's impossible. Somehow, somewhere, someone's going to be upset.

When the buzzer rings to let me know Tom's come to pick me up, I'm feeling more than a little relieved. My head's banging from trying to organise Cath's seating plan, and half a bottle of wine isn't helping matters. Cath buzzes him up, and I get up and open the door to let him in.

'Ah, got the right flat then,' Tom says as he reaches her floor and steps inside.

'If you didn't, then I didn't either,' I say, my little quip having sounded hilarious in my head but less so out loud. 'Tom, this is Cath. Cath, Tom.'

'Lovely to meet you, Tom,' Cath says. 'I've been hearing a lot about you.'

'Oh?' Tom says, looking at me. 'All good, I hope.'

'Of course,' I reply. 'I'm yet to discover the bad bits.'

'He hasn't told you that he's a psychopathic murderer yet, then?' Cath says, laughing. 'String of ex-girlfriends buried in the back garden?'

Tom doesn't seem to pick up on the humour. 'You ready, then?' he says.

'Uh, yeah. I think so.'

'Cool. I'll wait in the car, then.'

As Tom turns to leave, Cath calls out to him. 'Bye, Tom! Lovely to meet you!'

'Yeah, you too,' he says as he disappears back behind the door and down the stairs.

'He seems... nice,' Cath says, with a look on her face that tells me she's not being entirely honest.

5

'What was that all about?' I ask as we get into the car.

'Nothing. I just didn't think it was very funny, that's all.'

'She was only having a laugh,' I say. 'It's just her sense of humour. You'll get used to it.'

'Sorry, but it's not the sort of thing I find funny. You know what Erin did. It's not the sort of thing to joke about.'

'She doesn't know about that, Tom. I didn't tell her anything about Erin leaving you, obviously. And she wouldn't have joked about it if I had.'

Tom sighs. 'Alright. I said sorry. It was just a bit close to the bone for me, that's all. I'll apologise to her and explain. Did you get your planning done?' he says, changing the subject.

'Sort of. The seating plan's still causing problems. We need to get that all sorted before we can move onto anything else. She's still got some invitations that haven't gone out.'

Tom raises his eyebrows. 'She doesn't sound very organised.'

'She's not,' I say, chuckling. 'That's why she relies on me.'

Tom nods. 'Not too much, I hope?'

'I dunno. What's too much? Friends are supposed to rely on each other, aren't they?'

'Well, yeah, but not if one of them's taking advantage of that. As long as you aren't just working as a free wedding planner for her. Those people cost a bomb. I should know.'

'Did you and Erin have a wedding planner?' I ask.

'Yep. Cost an absolute fortune. And her only real skills were being organised and having some time on her hands. I can imagine it must be quite handy for her, having you as a friend.'

I sit and think about this for a moment. I'm not quite sure where all this has come from, but it does make me think. Cath does very little without me nudging or prompting. She's already miles behind in her wedding planning and she wouldn't be this far along the road if it wasn't for me.

'It's just what friends do,' I say. 'She's been there for me plenty of times. She's always a good listener and judge of character. Her instincts are always right. That's helped me out a lot over the years. We work well together.'

'Good,' Tom says, although I sense from the tone in his

voice that his reaction isn't altogether positive. 'Just as long as she's not taking advantage of you.'

I smile. It's sweet that he's looking out for me, but he really doesn't need to. Cath and I are chalk and cheese, but we've been close friends for years. She's always had my back, and it's encouraging to know that Tom has mine too.

UNTITLED

The monarch butterfly is a curious creature. As a caterpillar, it eats only milkweed — a plant that's poisonous to just about every other animal on the planet, but which forms the sole diet of the monarch caterpillar. They're completely dependent on this toxic plant.

Once it emerges from its chrysalis as a beautiful monarch butterfly, it no longer needs the poisonous milkweed. Not only that, but it has stored and channeled the poison into its wings — the very things that give it flight.

That's why the monarch is so successful. It's learned to not only ignore the poison and be unaffected by it, but to store it up and use it against its own predators.

We can take a lot of lessons from the monarch butterfly. It's a beautiful, delicate creature. It flutters silently through our gardens, not wanting to harm a soul, yet possessing the power to end lives.

Everyone always thinks they're good for people, but most don't realise they're toxic too. Like you, Catherine Baker.

I know who you are. I've done my research. Fortunately for me, you're one of those people who thrives on gushing their lives onto social media — without even bothering to lock down their privacy settings, of course. #unfortunate.

You're no good for Grace. You're toxic. You depend on her to carry out basic functions of your own life. You're pathetic. You're a drain on her soul.

Worse than that, I can see you're going to be a problem. Grace might think you've got good instincts, but I can promise you now they aren't a patch on mine.

If you were so perfect, she'd have been happy long before she met me. But she wasn't. She was missing something. She was missing me.

6

It's been a while since Cath and I have been out together for a drink. We used to do it regularly when we were younger, and again when Matt left and I needed the friendship — not to mention the alcohol. But things have died down on that front in recent months. I've not even seen her in almost two weeks, since the night we tried to fix her seating plan. I get it. I've been busy with work, she's been busy with the wedding preparations.

I've been seeing more and more of Tom, too. In fact, we've ended up spending most evenings together recently. It's faster than I'd usually move things, but it just feels right. It seems natural. That's why I invited her out tonight. Well, one of the reasons, anyway.

First, the topic of conversation turns to the wedding, as it always does.

'We *think* we might have finally sorted out the seating arrangements,' she says, suddenly producing a sheet of paper from the depths of her bag and thrusting it at me. 'What do you think? It should keep everyone happy, although there's probably something I've missed.'

'It looks good,' I say. 'Well done. Must be a load off your mind.'

'It's one load off it, yes. Plenty more where that came from, though. Just you wait until it's your turn. Shit. Sorry. That was insensitive. But no-one tells you how much people try to interfere and offer their thoughts and opinions all the time, even though they're telling you it's fine, it's your decision, it's your day, it's what you want that counts. But if you *could* just make sure this, that and this happens, everyone would be awfully grateful.'

I want to tell her that at least her fiancé is going to turn up on the day and not leave her with a fully-planned and mostly-paid-for wedding, not to mention a broken heart. I can't begrudge Cath feeling stressed out about it all, though. And I certainly can't begrudge her a lifetime of happiness.

Maybe a small part of her is acutely aware of the Matt situation and perhaps she's a bit worried the same might happen to her. She and Ben are devoted to each other, and it's never going to happen, but it's the sort of thing that would make anyone worry — even if only at the very back of their mind.

'Seriously, the thing I've learnt is to just nod and smile,' Cath says, as I realise she's going off on one of her reflective ramblings. 'Most of the time they forget the stuff they've mentioned anyway. They just want to suggest something, anything that makes them feel useful in some way, when what you actually want is to say "Bugger off and let me get on with it", but you can't say that because it's a wedding and everyone's meant to be happy and relaxed and everything's joyous and wonderful. I'll tell you what. There's a reason why people who get married a second time choose a cheap registry office and a reception in the pub afterwards. Sometimes I wish we'd decided to do that this time. You still end up with a ring on your finger and a certificate in your hand. And that way you've got an extra fifteen grand in your back pocket, too.'

'It's not all about money, though, is it?' I say. 'It's meant to be the biggest day of your life. You want to do it properly. No-one remembers the credit card bill twenty or thirty years down the line. They remember the photos, the event, the glamour. I know it's hard work now, but it'll all be worth it in the end.'

'So they keep telling me.'

It's strange seeing Cath like this. She doesn't tend to do stress. She's always the calm, level-headed one who is able to see both sides in any argument and always latches on to the positivity in all situations. She's not the sort of person to lose her head over something like this. I decide it might be best to change the subject.

'So things are going well with Tom. We seemed to have hit it off brilliantly. Just sort of clicked, you know?'

'I'm glad to hear it,' Cath replies.

'So, come on. What did you think of him? Honestly.'

'Honestly? Well, I didn't really get to see much of him. I thought his reaction was a bit... weird.'

'Yeah, sorry about that. It was all a bit of a misunderstanding. I don't think he took the comment about the exes too well. Between you and me, he was married before. She took off with the kid and all their money.'

'Jesus.'

'Yeah. Don't tell him I said anything, will you? It's not something he likes to talk about, for obvious reasons.'

'Of course not. I won't say a thing. He knows I was only messing around, right? And that I didn't know any of that?'

'Yeah, he does. He already said he was sorry. Just one of those things. Must've caught him in a bad mood.'

'Well hopefully I'll catch him in a better mood next time.'

'You will. I was thinking, maybe we can sort something out on that front. I was thinking about organising a night out or a meal or something. For the friends, I mean. It's been so long since we've caught up, and we only ever seem to do weddings and christenings.'

'There's the barbecue coming up.'

I chuckle. 'True. Might be nice to do something before that, though. Something that isn't just part of the annual routine.'

The barbecue is an odd tradition, but definitely one of my favourites. One of our friends, Gareth, moved here from

Australia a few years ago. He mentioned one time how Christmas in Australia was so different — mainly because it was the middle of summer over there. He said he missed having a barbecue on the beach, which was his traditional equivalent of our Christmas dinner. Ever since then, it's been our own annual tradition for a group of us to head to the seaside on the weekend before Christmas. It's always absolutely freezing cold, but that's part of the fun. It means we all get a short trip away, it gives us an excuse to catch up and Gareth gets his barbecue on the beach. We tend to get a few odd looks from passers by, but we have a lot of fun. The location changes every year, but this year it's Brighton.

'I'll arrange something,' I say, stirring my drink with my straw. 'If you're up for it, that is. Doesn't need to be anything big. Just a meal in a local pub somewhere. We should all make more of an effort to see each other.'

'Sounds good to me,' Cath says, shrugging her shoulders. 'You're not going to hear me complaining about a pub lunch. At least it makes all the "we should do this again soon" platitudes seem less false.'

'In fact, it'd be good to do that fairly soon, because I've been having a think about asking him to move in with me.'

Cath raises an eyebrow. Only enough to show interest, but I know Cath, and I know her instinct isn't that this is a great idea.

'Oh?'

'Well, he's been spending a fair bit of time at mine anyway,' I say. 'More and more, actually. And I'm relying on Mum and Dad to help me out with the mortgage still, and Tom's being put up in one of his boss's rentals, so it makes sense. I get some help with the bills, his boss gets his flat back, and we move things on to the next level.'

'Quite soon, though, isn't it?' Cath says, in a tone of voice which ensures the question answers itself.

'Maybe, but so what? If we click and we get on, what's the difference between now and six months' time?'

'Erm, because he might be a complete idiot who you don't want to live with?'

'In that case I'm better off finding that out sooner rather than later, aren't I?'

Cath cocks her head and raises her eyebrows briefly. 'I suppose that's one way of looking at it.'

'Anyway, it's not as if I'm going to be adding his name to the deeds or anything. It's just a bit of help contributing towards the bills, gives me some company and means we get to see if we're actually able to live together. Seems daft me floating around in there by myself, struggling to make ends meet while he's stuck in his boss's pokey flat.' I can tell by the look on Cath's face that she's really not keen on the idea. 'What is it?' I ask her.

'Nothing. I just think you're rushing into things, that's all.'

'Come on, Cath. I've been on my own for months. It's hardly rushing, is it?'

'Yeah, and the first bloke to come sniffing around gets moved in within a fortnight. I know the whole Matt thing ruined you, but I don't think this is the right way to get over it. You need to give yourself a bit more time. I don't want you getting hurt again, Grace. I'm just looking out for you, that's all.'

In that moment, I'm not sure I believe her.

7

When I get home, I call Tom. I just need someone who's on my side right now. I don't mention the conversation I had with her about him possibly moving in. As far as I'm concerned, she's ruined that for me and it's impossible to get excited about the prospect at the moment. All I can see is her disapproving face.

'How was it?' Tom asks.

'Oh, you know, the usual.'

'Did you pass on my apology for the other week? I still feel terrible about that.'

'I did. Apology accepted, she says. I think she's got bigger worries on her plate right now.' I figure it's best to make less of an issue out of it than it needs to be. Once Cath gets to know the real Tom, she'll have forgotten all about their first meeting. And Tom doesn't need to know about Cath's feelings. She doesn't even know him yet.

'Oh?' Tom asks.

'Don't worry. The usual pre-wedding dramas. The huge, massive problems which actually aren't an issue at all and which she won't remember in a year's time.'

Tom chuckles. 'She's probably just freaking out. It's a busy time. She wants everything to be perfect, I suppose. Can't begrudge her that.'

'I don't,' I say, perhaps a little too defensively. 'But that doesn't mean she needs to be a Bridezilla about it.'

'Oooh, I haven't heard that one before,' Tom says. 'I like.'

'What, Bridezilla? Come on, you must have heard that term.'

'To be honest, I tend to steer well clear of weddings these days.'

'Ah. Yeah. Sorry,' I say. Tom makes no mention of my almost-wedding, and this strikes me as perhaps a little insensitive, but I can't blame him for thinking of his own situation first.

'It's alright,' he says. 'I didn't mean it like that. We only had a small do, anyway. Village church ceremony, drinks reception at the village hall afterwards with a buffet. Not a whole lot to get worried about, really.'

I smile. 'Yeah, I think that's probably how I'd want to do it. Especially after seeing the way Cath's behaving over the Wedding of the Century.'

'Why? What sort of things is she doing?'

'Oh, just moaning basically. She's making mountains

out of molehills. Complaining about people offering to help, that sort of thing. She sounded a bit ungrateful if you ask me, especially after everything I've done to try and make it the best day of her life.'

'Like you say. Probably just the stress. She'll be fine after it's all done.'

'Yeah, I know. But that's not the point, is it? Weddings are a celebration. We want to be able to enjoy it with her.'

'As long as she isn't taking advantage of you. Did you know that weddings are one of the top reasons why friendships fall apart? I can definitely see why.'

'I know. I don't think it'll cause any long-term problems. Just got to look forward to it, I suppose.'

'I know,' he replies, and I can hear his smile. 'Just don't let it drive a wedge between you, alright? I don't want anything harming my butterfly.'

'Don't worry,' I say. 'I won't.'

8

It proved easier than I'd imagined to get everyone together for a meal and drinks, especially with so many people having work Christmas parties, family engagements and other stuff going on in the run-up to the festive season. In the end, today seemed to be the day most people could do, and we managed to get booked into a gastropub in a village a few miles outside town.

A couple of the guys come in ridiculous Christmas jumpers — something I get a laugh out of seeing others do, but wouldn't be seen dead in myself. The pub's nice enough, and is thronging with people in both the bar and restaurant.

'Lucky we managed to book a table,' Tom says as we get our drinks.

'It was the last one, apparently. They'd had a cancellation an hour or two before I called. Otherwise we'd have been totally stuffed.'

'Well, as long as the turkey has been too, I'm happy.'

Not long after, the others start to arrive. We arranged to meet in the bar half an hour before the table booking so we could have a drink while everyone arrives. Cath and Ben are the first, and we get a few minutes for Ben to meet Tom and introduce himself before the others turn up and we head to our table.

The food's delicious — far better than I expected, and I wonder if we might have found ourselves a hidden gem. What's more, the conversation is flowing and everyone seems to be getting on really well with Tom. It always amazes me how well he manages to turn on his charisma when he meets new people. It's almost like he's got a gift for it, and people are just naturally attracted to him as a person.

Tom and I are sat opposite each other, and Cath's sitting next to him, Ben on the other side, with Cath regaling Tom with her horror stories about the wedding planning, while I talk to Gareth and a couple of our other friends at the other end of the table. For the most part, I tune out of what Tom and Cath are saying. They seem to be getting on really well, and in any case I've heard it all before about how draining it is planning a wedding, how everyone interferes, how sometimes she wishes she'd never bothered. Ben catches my eye every now and again and gives me a knowing glance, and we both have a secret chuckle. A little while later, Tom says something which catches my attention.

'I just think you should go easy on her, especially considering the whole Matt thing,' are the words I hear.

I realise it's probably not something I was meant to pick up, but now I've heard it I can't help but tune in. It's almost as if everything else is silenced and my brain can focus only on what Tom and Cath are saying. I try desperately to listen to Gareth, Ben and the others, and I nod and smile along as they talk, but I don't hear a word of it. There's only one conversation I'm focused on.

'That was ages ago. And anyway, you don't know anything about it. You weren't even there.'

'No, but I've heard. It hurt her a lot, obviously, and has been really frustrating for her.'

'Yeah, well I've been under a lot of pressure myself recently, thank you very much.'

'Yeah, I know. She mentioned you'd been a complete and utter Bridezilla.'

As I hear those words, my heart lurches. My breath catches in my throat and I feel a cold shiver run down my spine. Cath looks over at me. She can see I'm a deer caught in the headlights, and in that moment I can see she knows immediately that what Tom's said is true. She doesn't say anything, though. She just looks at me, a picture of sadness and disappointment on her face.

9

A moment or two after Tom drops that clanger, Cath excuses herself and says she needs to go outside for some air. The only people who would have noticed this as being a bit odd were me and Ben, and Ben's busy in conversation with someone else and barely even notices her getting up. I can't leave things like this, so I follow her, out into the car park at the back of the pub. It's only when I step outside that I realise I've left my coat indoors, hanging over the back of my chair.

'Cath,' I say, walking up to her.

'*Bridezilla?* Why would you even say something like that?'

I can tell it's pointless even pretending I didn't. She'll have known from the look on my face at the table that it's true. I must have looked like a guppy fish, sitting there trying to work out what to say but floundering around, lost for words, the colour of beetroot.

'Cath, it's not like it seems. Tom heard the story second hand, and he must have got his words muddled up. He's just—'

'Oh really? Second hand? So you've been talking to other people about what a terrible person I am too, then, have you?'

'No! I haven't been talking to anyone. I just mentioned to Tom the other night that you seemed worked up about the wedding. It was just a totally normal conversation.'

'Grace, I've asked you for your help. I've gone along with all of your ideas. I haven't been worked up in the slightest.'

'I just... Tom asked what I was worried about, and I said that. I shouldn't have, but I did. So there we go.'

'I'm not worried about what you said or didn't say, Grace. That's not the point.'

'So what is the point?'

Cath shuffles from one foot to the other. 'It's Tom.'

'What about him? What's that meant to mean?'

'You know damn well what it means. He's wheedled his way in, earned your ear, now you're telling him all our private conversations. Is it any surprise I don't think it's a good idea to move him in with you? He's not right, Grace.'

'You mean he's not Matt.'

'That's uncalled for.'

'Is it?'

'Come on, Grace. How long have we known each other?'

'It's not about us, is it? It's about Tom. A guy you've spent ten seconds with in your life up until tonight.'

'As if you've spent any longer with him. And he's hardly coated himself in glory tonight, has he?'

I look at her for a few moments, not knowing quite what to say. 'It's not that simple,' I manage, eventually.

'Yes it is. When Tom was making those comments, there was something in his eyes. A glint. It was almost as if he was getting a kick out of saying those things, like he knew it was going to provoke a reaction.'

'I dunno,' I say. 'That doesn't sound much like Tom to me.'

'Yeah, that's what I'm worried about,' Cath replies. 'It's this "two sides" thing that concerns me. It might be nothing. I might be barking up the wrong tree completely. It's only because we're so close that I can talk honestly to you about it. I don't have a good feeling about Tom. Just be careful, alright?'

'Careful? Are you serious? You make it sound like he's dangerous and I'm foolish.'

'Yeah, well maybe that's not so far from the truth. I've warned you. That's all you need to know.'

'Right. If that's the way you want it to be, that's fine.'

'Yeah, well that's not the sort of things best friends do to each other, Grace. They tend not to stab each other in the back. Especially not after everything I've done to support you when you needed me. Thanks a lot. Thanks a fucking lot.'

With that, Cath turns and heads back inside the pub.

10

Cath and I sat in silence for the rest of the meal. Ben and Tom realised something was up, but it was pretty clear neither of us wanted to explain what had happened. Not in front of everyone else, anyway.

I didn't say a word on the drive home, either. Tom drove back — we'd planned for him to stay at mine tonight anyway — and he didn't push or make any attempt to force me to tell him what had happened. He seemed to get it, seemed to understand. And I reckon quite a big part of him knows it was stupid of him to have said such a thing.

'Look, I'm sorry,' he said, as he parked his car up outside my place.

'What for?' I say, knowing damn well what for but wanting to hear him say it.

'For the Bridezilla comment. I just—'

'Just what?'

'I don't know. I was just trying to defend you, that's all.'

'Defend me? Why the hell were you discussing me and Matt with her anyway? That's none of your business. You weren't even on the scene then. I managed perfectly well before you came along, so I don't need you defending me now.'

There's a look of sorrow on Tom's face. 'Sorry.'

'And what kind of idiot would mention the Bridezilla comment? What on earth possessed you to think she wouldn't fly off the handle when you told her about that?'

'I wasn't thinking. I'm sorry, I really am. I know you're capable of standing up for yourself, but I felt I needed to defend you. To keep you safe. She was saying things about you, and it didn't feel comfortable. I was just looking out for you.'

'Saying things? What was she saying?'

'It's nothing. Really. I'm sure she didn't mean it. I wouldn't want to cause any problems between you.'

'Tom. Tell me.'

Tom shuffles awkwardly in the car seat. I can tell he doesn't want the confrontation or drama. 'She just mentioned something about you being jealous about her wedding and things going well for her, that's all. Something about you not acting like you cared. I was just pointing out that you've had a lot on your plate. That's why I mentioned the Matt thing. I care about you, Grace. I know she's your friend and it's not my place to say anything, but it felt like she was attacking you. I'm sure she's just worked up about the wedding. I just wanted to be there for you, that's all.

I let out a huge sigh and rub my face.

'Yeah. I know. You don't need to say it. She was being a massive cow.'

We sit in the car for a moment, before Tom suggests we should head inside, as it's pointless sitting outside in the car.

When we get in, Tom makes me a cup of tea and we snuggle up on the sofa together.

'You know, Cath and I've never really had a falling out before. Not like that, anyway,' I tell him.

'It's bound to happen at tense times,' he replies. 'You've been through a lot recently. Plus you've got all the stuff going on with your nan. And she's got a wedding to organise, which can't be easy. Especially with Ben. He seemed a bit of a wet drip.'

'He is. They both are.'

Tom shrugs his shoulders. 'I'm not sure wedding planning's my sort of thing, either. There's something quite appealing about just grabbing a suit and turning up on the day.'

I nudge him playfully. 'Don't go getting any ideas. I'll want you making a full effort, thank you very much. You wouldn't want me going full Bridezilla on you, would you?'

Tom chuckles. 'No, I suppose not. Listen, Grace. I'm sure it'll all blow over at some point. She'll apologise. She has to, after behaving like that. You didn't do anything wrong.'

I shake my head. 'You don't know Cath. She's as stubborn as anything. There's no way she's going to be the one to make the first move.'

'Well, in that case I think that says it all about her. Everyone saw the way she acted tonight. If she can't even apologise to you for that, well...'

'Well what?' I ask.

'Nothing. I'm just saying she should be man enough to apologise, that's all. I mean, I know it's probably technically my fault, but...'

'No, no it wasn't. I don't hold you responsible, believe me. It's my fault for saying those things about her behind her back and her fault for flying off the handle at me. I'm not going to shoot the messenger, don't worry.'

'Good,' Tom says, pulling me in towards him. 'Because you know I'll always be there for you, don't you? Even when other people decide to act like divas and idiots. I'll always be the one that's here to support you, alright?'

I look at him and smile.

UNTITLED

That's the problem with sticking plasters. They might cover up the problem, but they don't solve it. And when you peel them off, they fucking hurt. It's always much less painful in the long-run if you rip them off quickly. The pain will be sharper, more intense, but it won't last anywhere near as long.

I'm only looking out for you. I only ever wanted you to be safe and happy — and mine. Nothing in life is ever simple. I accept that. I realise there are obstacles, things I need to remove before we can enjoy the life we were meant to.

This is the best thing for you, my butterfly. You know I only want the best for you, don't you? It'll hurt now, but it'll be good for you in the end. This is a long game. It's not about the here and now. Everything is a means to an end. And that end is us.

One of the perks of my job is that there's scope for working from home. Like most modern companies, 'scope' tends to translate to 'make sure you get the work done and don't take the piss'.

That policy was gratefully used this morning when Dad received a call from Nan's carers to say it looked as though she'd taken a turn for the worse. All we could work out was that she'd been rambling incoherently about Alfred the Great being in her wardrobe, and they wanted us to go over to see her and help calm her down.

It seems to have done the trick, and Mum and Dad are happy that she's back to normal — or as normal as she can be, anyway. We're all staying on high alert, and I've taken the day as a work-from-home day, just in case we need to go over again.

I open my email software and there's a message waiting from Matilda, the owner of the art gallery we had to organise the launch party for recently. The subject line is *A few things*, which immediately makes my heart sink. Whenever that woman has anything to say it's never good news, so the thought of her having a few things to say is frankly depressing.

Dear Grace, the email begins.

I wanted to write to you to convey a few concerns and disappointments I have following the recent launch event for X1.

As you were aware, anticipated numbers for the launch event were high, and for this reason I suggested early on in the process that it might be wise to stagger the times at which guests arrived. This was not done, and as a result we had high-class guests and dignitaries left queuing outside in the wind and rain for up to half an hour. I'm sure you will agree this is absolutely not acceptable.

We were also told that a high-profile celebrity would be on hand to conduct the official opening of X1. Whilst I accept that I did not follow up with you on who the specific celebrity would be, I did trust and have faith that you had this matter in hand, and was disappointed (to say the least) to discover that the best you could manage was Brian

Hapgood from 'Gold in the Garage'. That a large percentage of my personal guests were better known than him is testament to the sheer disbelief we all had at his attendance. I do hope he does not expect to be paid for this appearance.

Whilst we're on the subject of money, might I also add my disappointment at discovering a complete ignorance of the agreed budget. The maximum spend was stated quite clearly in our second email of the 14th, and I have no record or recollection of agreeing any increase in the budget — and certainly not an overspend of 14%!

Whilst I understand and accept that your expertise and experience in these matters are more than welcome, I am left feeling that the input and requirements of me — the customer — have been completely and utterly ignored.

I'm sure you will recall that the partners intend to open six X1 galleries across London within the next two years, and that we have some extremely high-profile and high-wealth backers. We had certainly intended to use your company to handle the launches of each of the galleries in our future portfolio, but this is now in serious jeopardy. A final decision has been put on hold whilst we await your comments on this matter.

Yours,

Matilda Dewitt.

P.S. Was there some confusion over the colour scheme? It was expected that you would be changing the colours from purple to white, as agreed in our emails on the 23rd of the month.

I sit and stare at the laptop screen, my jaw hanging as I try to comprehend what I'm reading. I go through it again, sure I must have misunderstood something somewhere along the line. But no, Matilda Dewitt actually is a complete and utter mental case.

I know at this point I should pause, make a cup of tea, jot down a few notes as to aspects that need to be addressed in a response and compose a calm, collected reply which covers the points she made in a professional and polite manner.

But — quite frankly — fuck that.

I compose a new email to Susan, my boss. Thankfully, we have a good relationship and can talk frankly and openly to each other. She's always got my back.

Hi Sue,

I'm guessing by now you'll have read the email from Matilda

@ X1. What a cow! I'm sure you know all the details by now, but anyway...

The bit about her suggesting staggering the times of arrival is an outright LIE. This was MY suggestion but she turned it down because she didn't want her snooty Z-list arse-lickers to get butthurt by being demoted to the second or third round of admissions. She even made some sort of snarky comment about them being 'dignitaries, not shift workers'. Snotty bitch.

When it comes to the weather, there was a LIGHT DRIZ-ZLE, which makes no difference anyway, because they were standing outside (for ten minutes at most) under a massive bloody awning! As for the wind, you'll note her husband's dodgy toupee managed to stay stuck to his head, so it can't have been that windy!

The celeb thing you already know about. I don't know what we can do about that, and I know you'll probably say we should just swallow the £500, but that doesn't sit right with me. She had HUNDREDS of chances to give me just SOME information on the sort of celeb she expected to open her shitty gallery, and she ignored me every time. If all of her friends are more famous, why didn't she ask one of them to get their bloody scissors out and cut the ribbon?

Budget... Jesus F* Christ. OBVIOUSLY it was over budget,

because she kept changing her sodding mind every five minutes and we had to pay for everything two or three times over! That's why some of the stuff was still purple, because there was no money left to change it all to white. Most of it had already been delivered and opened.

I know you'll probably want to pacify her in some way because of the future business stuff, and that's fine, but I just wanted to convey my thoughts to you, because I sure as hell can't bring myself to reply to that cow myself.

I'm WFH today, but back in the office on Monday or am on my mobile if you need to get hold of me. Advance warning: keep the volume turned down, because I'll be LOUD! Grrrr....

G x

*P.S.... * The F does not stand for Fred.*

As soon as I hit *Send* I know it probably wasn't a good idea, but sometimes these things need saying. Anyway, Sue and I get on really well and it wouldn't be the first time we'd slagged Matilda off behind her back. When you're dealing with people like that, sometimes you need a virtual punchbag to let out all the rage. It definitely feels much better for getting it all off my chest. At least now Sue will know how I feel and will be able to get that all across to Matilda in a way I know I'd never manage.

Now that's out of the way, I decide to make myself that cup of tea, take a moment to breathe and then get on with the rest of my work.

12

It's the day of the annual seaside trip for the beach barbecue, and we're all heading to Brighton. It wasn't until we'd all got our hotels and transport arranged that Ben decided to pipe up and mention that Brighton's got a pebble beach, not a sandy one. Trying to have a barbecue on a British beach in December is usually difficult enough in itself, but trying to lay down picnic blankets on loose pebbles and cobbles is going to add a whole new layer of interest.

That's not the only thing that seems to have caused some issues, though. Transport has also thrown a spanner in the works. There had been a big debate about which would be the best way to get to Brighton: road or rail. In the end, some people decided to go by train and the others wanted to drive. As it turned out, those of us who went by train somehow forgot to check for engineering works, and we ended up having to change trains twice, as well as lugging our bags through central London between stations. Fortunately for us, we got our schadenfreude when Melissa texted to say they were stuck in traffic because there'd been an accident and the M23 was shut.

At that point, I was just about ready to jump back on the train and go home. I've not been looking forward to it anyway, with Nan being so unwell and the argument between me and Cath still simmering away unresolved. It's not like us to ignore each other, but maybe that's what we both need right now. It's going to make today awkward, though.

Finally, eventually, we all arrive in Brighton. The others have parked up and are checking in at our hotel, a street or two back from the seafront, and we walk the short distance down the hill from the station to join them.

Gareth and Melissa have brought their two kids, and Cath and Ben have dragged Ben's niece and nephew along for the day to keep them company. Cath keeps nudging Ben and giving him little knowing smiles as the kids play in front of them, as if to say "That could be us soon!". Nauseating.

The weather's actually pretty good for December — the temperature's in double figures — and the wind isn't as ridiculous as I remember it tending to be in Brighton, from holidays as a kid.

When we get to the beach, Cath taps me on the arm. 'Grace, do you have a sec?' she says.

We walk a few yards off course, just enough to be able to talk in private.

'Look, I just wanted to clear the air so today isn't awkward,' Cath says. 'We both said things we didn't mean, and it's pointless there being bad blood between us. We've only got a few weeks left until the wedding, and I'd hate there to be bad feeling knocking about. For both our sakes.'

I force a smile. 'Thanks, Cath. I appreciate that. I'm sorry too.'

Gareth and Ben set up the portable, throwaway barbecues and fight to get them lit, while Cath, Melissa and I sit chatting as we watch Tom playing with the kids.

'He's great with them, isn't he?' Cath says.

'He is,' I reply. 'Gives us a bit of peace and quiet, too.'

'From them or from him?' she says, laughing.

'Both!'

'Aww, no, he's lovely. Bearing in mind he hadn't met any of the kids until half an hour ago, they're absolutely loving him.'

Melissa and I share a look. I know Cath probably doesn't mean what she's saying, and it's clear she's trying — perhaps a little too hard — to smooth things over and see the good in Tom. She obviously knows she's in the wrong, and at least she's making an effort.

'How's the wedding planning going?' Melissa asks, in a tone that's a little more probing than I'd expect.

'It's alright. Still a few things to sort out, but we'll get there,' Cath replies.

Melissa looks at me again and raises an eyebrow as if to say *Told you there's a reason she wants to make up with you.*

I look across the pebbles at the kids chasing Tom around, further towards the sea where the stones almost — almost — become sand. I can't hear what's being said, but there's plenty of laughing and shouting and everyone seems to be having a good time. Never mind Cath's knowing glances to Ben; as I look at Tom I get a glimpse of my own future. Maybe this is what it'll be like. Long, slightly warmer days, down on the beach, watching Daddy and the kids having fun in the sun.

In that moment, I feel sorry for Tom. For him, this must be both amazing and heartbreaking. Knowing that he can't have this sort of relationship with his own daughter must break him in two. Maybe that's why he gets on so well with other people's kids, I think. It's his way of getting that out of his system. And that's why I feel sorry for him: because he's a natural. He knows exactly what they want to do, precisely what they want to hear. He's got them engaged, enraptured and excited.

Twenty minutes or so later, Tom jogs back over to us to see how we're getting on.

'Yeah, not bad. Looks like you're keeping warmer than we are, anyway, all that running around,' I say.

'I was just going to ask if you wanted to come and look in a couple of shops with me, see if we can get some blankets or camping chairs or something,' Tom replies. There's a cheeky glint in his eye that tells me shopping's not all he's got planned.

'That sounds like a great idea,' I say, and I take his outstretched hand as he helps me up to my feet. 'Anyone want anything?'

'Nope, all good here,' Gareth says. 'Never too cold for a barbie.'

'Says the man who didn't know temperatures could drop below forty celsius before he moved to England,' Melissa says, laughing.

'Actually, Tom, there is something,' Cath says, looking at him. 'Ben and I have been doing a bit of shuffling around with the wedding plans. Looks like we got our numbers a bit mixed up, and there's a spare place. We wondered if you'd like to come.'

Tom looks at me, then back at Cath. 'Sure. That'd be really lovely. Thanks, Cath.'

13

Tom and I head off towards the road, holding hands as we clamber over the pebbles, my toes cold and numb inside my boots. Even though it's not a particularly cold day, sitting around on the seafront doing nothing isn't keeping me especially warm.

'You cold?' Tom says, feeling me shiver.

'A bit. I'll be alright after a walk.'

'Never mind a walk. Come on, this way,' he says, pulling me across the road and up a side street. A couple of minutes later, we walk into a kids' play park. There's no-one around, and it strikes me that slides, swings and round-abouts probably aren't massively popular in the middle of December.

'This should keep you warm,' he says, hoisting himself up and climbing along the monkey bars like a chimpanzee.

'I doubt it. That metal looks freezing!'

'Should've brought your gloves,' Tom replies, sticking his tongue out at me, making me laugh.

'You told me it wouldn't be cold enough for gloves.'

Tom shrugs. 'What can I say? I lied.'

'You're a bad man, Thomas.'

'Oh yes. Dreadful. Now are you going to just stand there or are you going to come and play?'

'That all depends what we're playing with,' I say, walking over to him, pressing my body up against him and kissing him. I feel like I'm fourteen again, stealing a snog in the park while my friends wait round the corner. For the first time in a long time, I feel free and secure at the same time. I love watching Tom mess around like a big kid, embracing his inner child while still making me feel so safe at the same time.

'Come on. Roundabout time!' Tom says, as he starts jogging over towards it, still holding my hand. 'On you get.'

'Okay, but be careful,' I say, giggling. 'I don't want to be sick.'

'You've only had two drinks.'

'Three. And I don't do well with motion at the best of times.'

'You could've fooled me,' he replies, flicking his eyebrows upwards seductively.

'Yeah, well it's been a long time since *that*'s happened anywhere near a play park,' I say, with false coyness.

Tom leans in close. 'We could always rectify that situation.'

As I move forward to kiss him, he pulls back and grins, before the roundabout starts moving.

'Tom!'

'Hold on tight!' he says, as he starts to spin it faster and faster. Every half-second or so I catch a glimpse of his face as I spin round past him. I don't know if I'm imagining things, but every time I see it the smile seems to drop slightly, until it's neutral, then almost angry.

'Tom, stop,' I say. 'It's too fast.'

He's not listening to me.

'Tom, I want to get off. I feel sick!'

I try to stand up, but the force keeps pushing me back down. I grip the metal safety bar and hoist myself round, before waiting for my moment and stepping off. The second I do so, I regret it. My right foot hits the ground and I stop, but the roundabout keeps spinning and I feel a searing pain as the metal bar smashes into my left shin, knocking me off balance and sending me into the sandpit.

I lie there for a moment or two, shocked and in pain, before Tom comes over.

'Jesus, Grace. Are you alright? Why'd you just jump off like that?'

'I... I felt sick,' I say. 'I asked you to stop... Fuck that hurts!'

'Where does it hurt?' Tom says, lifting up my trouser

leg. 'Oh wow. You've got quite a bruise there already. You'll want to keep that covered up.'

'Why didn't you stop when I asked?' I say, trying to catch my breath as the pain slowly begins to subside.

'I didn't hear anything, babe. Honestly. If I'd heard you say stop, I would've stopped. You know that, don't you?'

I look up at him, and there's a look in his eyes I can only describe as neutral. It gives me nothing, but at the same time that's exactly what I find most disconcerting.

'Yeah,' I say. 'I know.'

I push myself to my feet, fighting against the horrendous pain in my leg, but knowing nothing is broken and I need to get it moving.

I start walking in the direction of the seafront, Tom following a few steps behind me. Neither of us says a word as we walk.

As we get back to the others, Cath calls out to us.

'Any luck?'

'Nope,' Tom says, before I can answer. 'Had a quick look around, but I don't think there's much call for chairs and blankets round here.'

'Probably because we're the only buggers daft enough to sit on the beach in December,' Cath says, laughing.

Tom heads straight back over to play with the kids, and the adults smile as they watch him, the sound of joyous laughter mixing with the crashing waves.

'I don't know where he gets his energy from,' Cath says to me, 'but I'm pretty sure you're not complaining.' As she chuckles, she notices some dirt on my jeans. 'Well well well. No wonder you didn't find any chairs or blankets, you dirty little buggers. I bet you're both warmed up too, eh?'

I force a smile and a small laugh. It's not ideal, but it's better than telling her the truth.

14
WEDNESDAY 25 DECEMBER

It's odd that Christmas Day should feel different from any other day, but it does. When all's said and done, it's just another day. The birds see the sun rise again, the dogs expect another walk, the trees are glad for another extra couple of minutes of sunshine compared to the day before. To all intents and purposes, it's just another Wednesday. But it's not. It feels warmer, cosier.

Maybe it's being around family. Perhaps it's a throw-back to childhood, when Christmas was undeniably a very different day to any other, when we'd wake up to the sound of Christmas songs, rush downstairs and rip open the presents while the smell of roast turkey wafted through the house. There was a wonder, an amazement which can't ever be replicated in adulthood, but of which we're reminded every Christmas Day. The annual muscle memory reminding us that this day *is* different.

The thing I always notice is the smiles. Of course, Mum and Dad are happy to see us whenever we go over, but Christmas Day seems to get you a bigger smile on arrival. It's not just a case of opening the door and letting you in; it's warmer, more welcoming. It means more.

Mum's always done a brilliant job of making Christmas feel relaxed, even though we know she's running around the kitchen like a blue-arsed fly. This year is different, though.

Everyone was agreed that we should enjoy Christmas as we always do. If Nan thought we were moping about, waiting for the call to say she'd died, she'd flip her lid without a shadow of a doubt. But it's clear we all feel slightly guilty each time we smile, as if we should be in a period of pre-mourning. But Christmas is a time for family, and for being together, and we should be able to enjoy that without feeling guilty.

Today of all days, I'm thankful for Tom. He's fortunate enough to be one step removed, close enough to know the situation and the dynamic, but also able to put some perspective on things and allow us to enjoy the day without feeling that he has to keep a lid on things.

It's at times like this that I realise how lucky I am to have him. Tom's at his best when he's like this. He's kind. He's supportive. He's a rock. He's everything the family man should be, and a family man always shines at Christmas.

He's taken it upon himself to be the unofficial drinks

waiter, making sure everyone's glasses keep topped up — one of the prerequisites of any good Christmas Day. Mum's banished him from the kitchen — along with everyone else — and has declared that the next person to ask if she needs a hand with anything will provide an uncomfortable new home for the turkey giblets.

I try to give Tom a knowing look to tell him that maybe it's not a great idea to keep topping Dad's glass up. He's already slurring his speech and getting short-tempered. After everything that's been going on with Nan he's not been in the best of moods lately, and I worry that he's going to act up.

We open a few presents and have a good laugh at some of the jokier gifts we've got each other. As a family, we've always been fortunate enough to buy the things we want throughout the year, so Christmas for us has always been about lighthearted gifts or those saw-this-and-thought-of-you items. After all, they mean so much more than a bottle of perfume or a necklace — no matter how sweet the scent or large the ruby.

After an hour and a half or so, we realise Mum's been stuck in the kitchen on her own, and decide on a plan to rescue her. We daren't offer her any help, but we can definitely insist she stops cooking for a few minutes and comes into the living room to open a few presents of her own. It is Christmas, after all.

Dad draws the short straw and heads out to the kitchen. A few seconds later, he comes back into the living room.

'Where is she?' he asks.

'I thought she was in the kitchen,' I say. 'Maybe she's gone upstairs to the loo.'

Dad heads upstairs, calling for her, and we think no more of it. A couple of minutes later, they come thundering down the stairs and round into the kitchen. We hear raised voices, and I stand up to see what's going on, but Tom placates me.

'It's alright. I'll go,' he says.

After a minute or so, Dad comes into the living room with a look of thunder on his face.

'Well that's the dinner fucked,' he says.

'What do you mean?'

'Your mum decided to fall asleep upstairs, didn't she. God knows why she didn't just ask one of us to keep an eye on things for a few minutes. Daft woman. Too bloody proud for her own good.'

Mum enters the living room, Tom walking closely behind her with a hand on each of her shoulders.

'We're alright, I think,' Tom says. 'It's salvageable.'

'Mum, what happened?' I ask.

'She had a bit of a funny turn,' Tom says. 'She felt like she needed to lie down for a minute, and seems to have dozed off. It's alright, it happens.'

'Are you okay now?' I ask Mum.

Mum nods.

'She'll be fine,' Tom says. 'I'll keep an eye on things in

the kitchen. Most of it's nearly ready anyway, so I can finish off the last few bits.'

'Most of it's bloody burnt, you mean,' Dad says.

'It'll be fine,' Tom replies.

True to his word, fifteen or twenty minutes later we're called through to the dining room and Tom serves up the perfect Christmas Dinner. I look at Mum and smile. She looks embarrassed, ashamed almost.

'Thank you, Tom,' she says, eventually. 'This is lovely.'

'Nonsense,' Tom says, pouring out the red wine. 'You did all the hard work. I just dished it up.'

It's agreed amongst us that it really doesn't matter who gets the credit, but that we're all enjoying the meal.

When dinner's finished, we're all suitably stuffed and decide to give it an hour or two before worrying about dessert. The thought of adding more food to my stomach is enough to make me feel ill, and I'm pretty sure I'm not going to want to eat for a week.

Instead, Dad and Tom pick out a board game while Mum and I load the dishwasher and tidy up in the kitchen.

'I don't know what happened,' she says, drinking a pint of water. 'I just came across all funny and knew I needed to lie down. I could have sworn I turned the hob off and the oven right down.'

'Honestly, don't worry about it. Everything was fine in the end. It was probably just the stress of trying to get everything ready, the heat in the kitchen, drinking on an empty stomach, who knows? Doesn't really matter now. But for Christ's sake tell us if you feel like that again, alright? There's no need to go sneaking off upstairs. You're too proud.'

'I know, I know. It was only meant to be for a minute or so. I must have just nodded off. I think maybe I had a little too much to drink. I didn't think I'd had that much, but I must've done.'

'Mum, forget it. Please. It's Christmas Day, and no-one else is bothered, believe me. We're all having fun.'

'Your dad isn't. He thinks I'm a silly old fool.'

'No he doesn't. Dad's just being Dad. Let's enjoy the rest of the day. Yes?'

Mum forces a smile and nods. I think she knows she doesn't really have much choice.

We head through to the living room, and find Dad and Tom sitting in silence. I don't know what they've been talking about, but it certainly seems as if the conversation is very much over now.

'Thought you were never coming out of there,' Dad says, nodding his head towards the kitchen.

'We were sorting out the mess from dinner,' I say.

'Well don't worry about all that. That can be done later.'

'It's done now.'

'Great. Now are we going to play this bloody game or what?'

Tom and I share a look — one that tells me Dad's been a right bundle of laughs while Mum and I were in the kitchen — and Tom starts to deal out some coloured cards, explaining the rules as he goes. I try to follow what he's saying, but I get lost a couple of times. I usually tend to work these things out much better by playing a round or two, rather than trying to understand everything that's being said.

After a few minutes, Dad's even more frustrated.

'I can't get a bloody word of this,' he says. 'I need a drink.'

'Maybe it's better if you read the rules, Grace,' Tom says. 'I'm clearly not doing a great job of it. I'll help your dad with the drinks.'

As Tom leaves the room, Mum and I try to decipher the rules of the game with no enthusiasm whatsoever.

A minute or so later, we hear raised voices and banging. Mum and I look at each other, then get up and rush into the kitchen, where we find Dad pinning Tom up against the radiator, before he lands a punch on his face.

'Dad!' I yell, before a second punch lands. 'What the fuck's going on?'

I rush over to Tom, checking his face.

I look at my dad, his eyes full of rage, and in that moment I feel like I don't know him anymore.

15

I spend the whole journey home mortified. Hurt. Broken. I've never seen Dad behave like that before. It was like a switch had flipped. I know he's been upset over the situation with Nan, and Christmas can often be like a tinderbox at the best of time, but none of that excuses what he did. Not by a long stretch.

'Are you going to tell me what the hell happened?' I ask Tom once we're back in the car.

'It's nothing,' he says. 'I probably deserved it.'

'What did you say to him? Why did he hit you?'

'I don't know. We were talking about your mum and her funny turn. I was worried about her. I mentioned that she was taking too much on and probably needed to see a doctor. Your dad said not to be so ridiculous and that it was Christmas. I was just concerned about her, that's all. She wasn't standing up for herself, and I felt that someone needed to defend her and look out for her. He wasn't.'

'Did you tell him that?'

'Not in so many words. I think he took it as if I was blaming him or something. I don't think I crossed a line, but maybe he saw it differently. Maybe I didn't put it across in the best way. He's obviously really worried about her too.'

'That's no excuse for hitting you, Tom,' I say.

By the time we get home, my jaw aches from how heavily I've been grinding my teeth. My chest is tight and all I can think of is how angry and disgusted I am with him. Sure, Tom wasn't exactly an angel, but he was Mother fucking Teresa compared to the way Dad reacted.

Tom, bless him, jumped straight to Dad's defence and tried to excuse what had happened. Not in front of him, of course. That would have been too awkward. But in the car on the way back, and now that we're home, he's been trying to play it down. It isn't working.

'Let's just try not to let it ruin Christmas, alright?' he says as I fumble with the key to unlock the front door. I'm still shaking with rage.

'I think it's a bit late for that,' I say, my voice faltering.

'I'm sure he didn't mean it. We'd all had a bit to drink, feelings were running high, these things happen. I'm sure he'll be apologetic in the morning.'

I make a snorting, huffing sound as I finally manage to wrestle the door open. 'I doubt that very much. You don't know my dad.'

'No, but I know that people often calm down overnight and see things differently. And I know that good men know when they've done something out of the ordinary and are quick to try to put it right.'

'You're assuming he's a good man,' I say, throwing my handbag down and closing the door behind us.

'I'm sure he is,' Tom says. 'That's why I'm certain he'll phone up tomorrow to apologise. But for now, let's just sit down and watch whatever shite's left on telly, shall we?'

I look at him, both in admiration at his nobleness and slightly enamoured by his naïveté. It's sweet of him, but also foolish to think that Dad's going to be anything other than the stubborn old bastard he's always been. Dad's never changed his mind or apologised for anything, and he's not about to start now.

'You should put some ice on that,' I say, gesturing toward Tom's lip.

'Probably a bit late for that now,' he says, dabbing at it with the back of his hand. 'At least it's stopped bleeding.'

'It'll be sore tomorrow.'

He smiles. 'I'm pretty sure I'm not the only one who'll be waking up with a sore head.'

'No, but at least you'll be waking up with a clear conscience.'

'It'll all blow over,' he says, walking through into the living room. 'He didn't mean it. It was just an overreaction. He's obviously just worried seeing you with another guy, after what happened with Matt.'

I shake my head. 'That was ages ago. It's no excuse. If I'm over it, he should bloody well be over it.'

Tom shrugs. 'Maybe it's just a dad thing. We find it harder to get over stuff.'

This stops me in my tracks momentarily. I keep forgetting Tom's got a daughter of his own, and that he probably sees things differently because of that. Especially considering he doesn't get to see her.

'Maybe,' I say.

'He's probably just worried because things aren't necessarily going how he expected.'

'How do you mean?'

Tom sits down on the arm of the sofa, next to me. 'Well, look at it this way. You've always been a pretty close family. He liked Matt, assumed you'd always be together, treated him like part of the family. Then... well, you know.'

'I know.'

'Can I ask you something?'

I nod.

'When you think back now, did you ever have suspicions about Matt? Not suspicions. Worries, perhaps. With the benefit of hindsight, do you think there might have been some signs as to what was to come?'

I think about this for a moment. 'Honestly?' I say. 'Probably. Yes. I think I knew for a long time his heart wasn't in it, but I didn't want to admit it to myself. Or to anyone else.'

Tom nods slowly. 'I thought as much. People do know.

Deep down, I mean. You like to please people and keep the peace, and that's great, but sometimes you've got to follow your gut and stand on your own two feet. If you'd listened to yourself about Matt, yeah, things still wouldn't have ended brilliantly, but you wouldn't have got so close to the wedding and been so ruined by it all. You probably wouldn't have wasted all that money either. But you wanted to listen to everyone else instead. You worried about what your parents would think, what other people wanted. You need to stop doing what other people think you should do and stand up for yourself.'

'Maybe.'

'There's no maybe about it. Every time you've not followed your gut, something bad has happened and you've suffered for it, all because you chose to listen to others over yourself.'

I think about this for a moment, and realise he's right. I worry too much about what other people think. But I'm not meant to be living my life for them; I'm meant to be living it for me.

'Yeah. I know,' I say. 'You're right.'

'I usually am,' he replies, with a cheeky grin on his face. He always knows just what to say to cheer me up, bring me back round and leave me feeling stronger.

'Yeah, well you can bask in the glory, mister. I'm going to take this as my opportunity to live life for myself. Well, I'm going to have a bloody good go at it, anyway.'

'That's my girl,' Tom says, winking.

'And I think I know the perfect way to get that party started.'

UNTITLED

They say that blood's thicker than water, but that's just not true. Toxic people are toxic people, regardless of who they shagged thirty-odd years earlier.

You can't choose your family. And that's why nobody needs them. In fact, they're the least important people in your life purely because you didn't choose them. They should have to work extra hard for your affections.

You're better off without them. I should know — I'm just fine without mine. I never felt I needed them, and I didn't feel bad once I was finally free of them. Why should I have? They were toxic. No-one regrets getting rid of poison.

I'm just glad you finally got to see what your family are like. A few drinks usually helps. In vino veritas, as the old saying goes. In wine there is truth. And gin. And whisky. Especially when they're served in double — or even triple — measures.

I'm pleased I did my bit. I'm happy to have helped you see the light. You don't need them. You never needed them, and you certainly don't now I'm here.

I'm proud of your decision. I'm proud of you. Proud of us. From now on, it will always be us.

16
THURSDAY 26 DECEMBER

Tom's made me see a lot of things differently. For all his sweet remarks about how Dad probably didn't mean to hit him, how everyone's just been stressed recently and he's sure it'll all blow over sooner or later, there was one comment that really stood out. It was the mention of standing up on my own two feet and saying 'sod it' to everyone else.

Even though it's the way I've always lived, I'm sick of people constantly telling me what I should or shouldn't be doing. Tom's right. I've always been too slow to stand up to people, and much preferred to keep everybody happy by just going with the flow. And where's that got me? Thousands of pounds in debt with a fiancé who fucked off and left me two weeks before our wedding, in a house I can barely afford with a job I'm getting sick to death of and a family who can't accept the one choice I've actually made for myself recently.

I look around at everyone else living the life they want and I'm sick of it. My friends all seem to be doing really well. They're getting married, having kids and I'm left suffering because I've spent my whole life listening to them instead of myself. And even though they get to live their perfect little lives, they still whinge about it. Cath can't help but complain about people wanting to help make her perfect white wedding even better. She's more than happy to slag off her loved ones, who genuinely want to lend a helping hand, but the second someone calls her out on that *they're* the bad guy.

Tom was wrong on one thing, though. There's no way in hell Dad's ever going to apologise for what he did, or even be the first one to make contact. Every ounce of his being will expect me to phone up, cap in hand, full of apologies and wanting to put it behind us. And, for a moment or two, I might just let him labour under that misapprehension.

I call the landline number for Mum and Dad's house, and wait for an answer. After a few seconds, Dad picks up.

'Hello?' His voice is clear and jolly.

'Dad. It's me,' I say.

'Oh. Hello.' He drops an octave and pushes as much disappointment through the phone line as he possibly can. Just as I expected.

'I just wanted to give you a call after what happened

yesterday,' I reply. This is where he's going to expect me to say sorry on behalf of Tom, to tell him I want to forget it all and move forward because *it's so much easier when everything's nice.* 'It made me think,' I say. 'And I've come to a decision. Frankly, I'm sick of constantly being pushed around by people trying to tell me what's best for me. There's only one person who gets to decide that, and that's me. I'm in charge of my own life, my own destiny, and if you're not going to accept that and support me, that's fine.'

Dad makes a huffing noise at the other end of the phone. 'Well you won't be wanting the money we put into your account each month to keep a roof over your head, then, will you?'

'No. You're right,' I say, before I can even think about the words that are coming out of my mouth. 'If you're not going to support my decisions and accept that I'm an adult and get to decide my own future, I don't want your money. I don't want a penny of it. If that's your attitude, go ahead and cancel the standing order. I'm not interested.'

Dad's a stubborn old bastard, but I get the feeling that if the shit were ever to really hit the fan, he might finally relent. Even knowing how obstinate and headstrong he is, I still don't expect to hear the response that comes out of his mouth.

'Alright. Fine. I'll do that now. Was there anything else?'

'No,' I say, trying to answer quickly and not leave any

form of silence that might indicate the slightest level of doubt or hesitation on my part. 'No, nothing else.'

'Bye then,' he says, and the line goes dead.

I look at Tom, unsure as to what my future holds, but knowing it's right there in front of me. He steps forward, pulling me into him, and now my future is holding me.

17

It's a big moment for me. I've always been close to my parents, and having a conversation like that is huge. We've never really fallen out before, mainly because I've always gone along with whatever they've wanted and have never really put my head above the parapet and gone my own way.

Tom tells me it's just the shock of things, and that they'll come round eventually. At the end of the day, he says, who wants to lose their only daughter over something so silly and trivial? Lots of people get through lots worse.

We sit on the sofa and I lean into him, my head on his shoulder as his hand caresses my hip.

'You know I'll do what I can, don't you?' Tom says. 'To support you. I mean, there's not a whole lot I can do financially, but I'll do what I can.'

'I know. But you don't need to do that,' I say.

'No, but I'd like to. I hate seeing you like this. I'm due a pay rise at some point, so I'll have a word at work. I can probably spare a little bit, but I don't know if it'll do much good. It's paying for that bloody flat every month that's doing it. You'd think he'd give me mates' rates or something, but no. It's sucking me dry.'

Tom puts the TV on and we flick through the channels, trying to find something that isn't a repeat of a Christmas special from a decade or two earlier.

Boxing Day is usually spent with my parents. We'll either meet for drinks in a pub somewhere or go for a walk. But this year that isn't happening. Yesterday's antics and my conversation with Dad this morning have probably put paid to that little family tradition. Short of a miracle, I can't see that happening again.

Right now, I'm not even at the stage of feeling bad about it. If he's upset, fine. He stepped a long way over the line and has one hell of a lot of work to do before I let him back into my life. I'm not budging on that. What worries me most right now is money.

I've been struggling with money for a while. Mum and Dad's contribution to the mortgage went a long way to just ensuring I could make ends meet, and without that I'm going to be completely and utterly lost. There's no way I'm going to qualify for any credit cards, especially seeing as I'm struggling to repay the ones I've got. And getting into even more debt is hardly going to improve things for me. As far as I can see it, I've only got one option.

It seems mad. Crazy. But I can't pretend the thought hasn't crossed my mind before. Of course it has. Everyone visualises the future, tries to imagine themselves married to the person they're with. They picture their kids, the Sunday mornings at the park, the years stretching out ahead of them. Right now, I just want to make it through the next year without being kicked out onto the street. And me and Tom taking our first steps together would be the perfect way to do that.

'I know it's only early days,' I say, 'but would you want to stay here more permanently?'

'Permanently?' he asks. 'You mean move in?'

'Well, yeah. I guess. I mean, I'm here on my own, you're staying in your boss's flat. You said yourself that you're paying through the nose for that place, even though it's not yours and you don't really want to be there. It seems a bit daft, really. Especially if you've been spending some nights here anyway.'

'Are you sure that's what you want? I mean, I don't want things to move too fast for you.'

'It's not too fast if we're both comfortable, though, is it?' I say.

'Well, no, but I just mean I wouldn't want you to have any expectations after everything that happened with Matt. I don't want you to feel like you have to do this because of the situation with your dad.'

'It's not,' I say. 'It's because I want you to live here with me.'

He pulls his arm away from me and sits up straight, looking me in the eye. He looks as if he's about to cry.

'Seriously, Grace, that would be amazing. I'd love that. Me and my butterfly.' He pulls me into a hug and kisses the top of my head. 'I want to pay my way, though. I'll contribute half of everything. Mortgage, council tax, bills, the lot.'

'You don't need to do that,' I say, secretly grateful that he's offered. There's no way I'm asking my parents to keep picking up the tab while I've got Tom stowed away here permanently. Certainly not after what happened yesterday. There's no way I'm going back on my word.

'I know, but I want to. It's only fair. It's what any gentleman would do. And I'm genuinely so grateful, Grace. I'm so happy to have met you.'

He leans in and kisses me. I reciprocate.

'You know,' he says, looking deep into my eyes. 'I don't think I've ever felt this way about anyone. I think I'm falling in love with you.'

I look back at him, half of me melting at his words and the other half panicking that this is coming on too soon. We've only been together a few weeks. The living arrangements were more of a practical suggestion than an offer to spend the rest of our lives together. But there's a big part of me that knows this guy is special. He's not like anyone else I've ever met. I can't keep comparing him to Matt. He isn't Matt. He'll never be Matt. And that's probably a good thing. Tom won't leave me practically standing at the altar.

'I'll get everything sorted out this week' he says. 'In terms of the money, that might have to wait a couple of weeks. I'm in the middle of changing banks at the moment and waiting for a big bonus from work. Ten grand, though, so that'll sort everything out. Is that alright?'

I force a smile. 'Sure,' I say. 'No problem.'

18

SATURDAY 28 DECEMBER

Tom's started moving some of his things in over the past couple of days, and everything should be out of his boss's flat by New Year.

'I spoke to him earlier, actually. I meant to say,' Tom tells me. 'He's going to check the rental contract, but there's a good chance I might have to pay up until the end of January as I officially need to give a month's notice.'

'That's a bit harsh, isn't it? I mean, he's supposed to be helping you out. I'm pretty sure he'd be able to find someone else to take the flat on before then.'

Tom shrugs. 'Yeah, I know. Like I say, he's happy to help me out with it, but I suppose it's only fair to want what it's worth. If I wasn't renting it, someone else would. It's not right that he has to lose money over it.'

'No, but still.'

'I'm sure we can sort something out if he finds a new

tenant sooner. I'll talk to him about it. Just letting you know, just in case.'

'Does that mean you might not be able to contribute to the mortgage until the end of next month?' I ask.

'I hope that won't be the case. Like I say, I'm sure we can sort something out long before then. Just didn't want to spring it on you at the last minute if it doesn't quite work out how we want it. Anyway, it's only temporary. We're due to complete on that project in China mid-January, and we'll be getting pretty hefty bonuses once that goes through so I can settle everything up then. You won't be out of pocket. I could probably even pay for a couple of extra months in advance.'

'So work's going well, then?' I ask, trying to change the subject to something a little more positive.

Tom takes a deep breath. 'Sort of, yeah.'

'Sort of?'

'Well, I was trying to find a way to tell you, but we think we're going to have to let some people go from the China contract. Some of the engineers and techies, I mean. They're not pulling their weight.'

'Oh. That's a shame,' I say.

'Yeah. Problem is, these guys have got no chance of finding another job around there. There's nothing like this at all. Not for a British company, earning that sort of money. It's the sort of thing that sets someone up for life over there. Foreign money. Puts kids through university, the lot. There are going to be some really unhappy people.

Organised crime and corruption's rife, too, so we've got to be really careful.'

'Careful how?' I ask, suddenly worried.

'We've been advised to take down our social media accounts. Just in case.'

'What, why?'

'Because things are different over there, Grace. If you think money talks over here, you wait until you see China. You don't just let people go from their jobs and expect nothing to happen. I'm just trying to protect you, that's all.'

And that's when it sinks in. 'Me? What do you mean protect me? I haven't done anything.'

Tom sighs. 'This is how their minds work. The risk is probably low, but I don't want to take any chances. I don't want them harassing you or causing you any issues.'

'Why would they?' I ask.

Tom sighs again. 'Look, they're not just being let go because they're useless. They're dodgy people. They can't be trusted. We've found out some things about them which should have been done on the background checks, but weren't. Because of what we do, providing security systems, we can't have people like that on the team. It's far too risky. It could be the end of our company. They're being let go while I'm over here,' he says, looking at his watch. 'Probably about now, actually. We know they have links to organised crime, but we don't know how deep or far those links go, and I don't think it's worth risking anything for the sake of a social media account, do you?'

I look at Tom's face. He seems genuinely worried and concerned — and slightly guilty for having to inconvenience me. It's not his fault if the company messed up, or they've got to let people go because they're linked to criminals.

'No, no I guess not,' I say. 'What's got to go? Facebook?'

'Facebook, Twitter, Instagram, the lot. Take them offline for now, as that's just easiest. I'll have a bit more of a look into it when things calm down. I think we can change names and things like that, which might be a better idea in the long run.'

'I'll try,' I say. 'But you might have to help me.'

'Yeah, of course. No problem. And look, I'm sorry. I know it's a pain in the arse. You know I'm just trying to keep you safe, don't you?'

I look at him and smile.

'Yeah. I know.'

19

One of the downsides about that weird bit in between Christmas and New Year is that no-one is ever quite sure what day it is. There's definitely one huge benefit, though: lie-ins. Until this morning, that is.

I must have been sleeping pretty lightly, because I'm woken by my phone vibrating on the bedside table as a text arrives. Bleary-eyed, I look at the screen. It's Dad.

I swipe to unlock my phone and read the message properly, although I've already got a fairly decent idea.

Dad doesn't usually text — he phones. If he's taken the time to tap out a text message one letter at a time, it's obviously something he wants to have some space to think over, without jumping to a reaction and saying something he'll regret. Most likely, Mum's there with him, helping him compose a reply between the two of them — something they wouldn't be able to do on a phone call or face-to-face.

Grace I just wanted to make things up with you. I know you want to go your own way and be independent and we both totally support you on that. That's fine. I just wanted to let you know that we're both still here for you, whenever you need it, for anything at all. OK? Love D x

I read the message a couple of times, half expecting to find some hidden barbs in there somewhere, but this seems to be from the heart. It's unlike Dad to back down like this, so it's clear to me that Mum's had a say in things. I note that he hasn't actually apologised for what happened, though.

I take a few minutes to compose my reply before sending it.

Thank you. I appreciate that, and will let you know if I need anything but I'm pretty sure I'll be fine. Did you also mean to add that you were sorry for punching Tom?

I hope that doesn't sound too inflammatory, but at the same time I want to make it clear that Boxing Day wasn't just a flash in the pan and that I'm serious about wanting to be independent and make my own decisions. I need to show some strength and resilience of my own.

Tom stirs beside me, realising I'm already awake. 'Morning,' he says.

'Morning.'

'Everything okay?'

I hand him my phone, watching him peer at the screen as he adjusts his eyes to the brightness.

'Blimey,' he says. 'Bet you weren't expecting that.'

'Yes and no.'

'Thoughts?'

I take a deep breath and let it out. 'I dunno. He's clearly trying to do the right thing, but I'm not entirely sure he's going about it the right way. Story of his life.'

Tom lets out a chuckle. 'Well, let's see what he says back to that. That'll be most telling.'

It's a few minutes before Dad's reply pings through to my phone.

You know I am. I'm trying to mend bridges now. The standing order has been cancelled but I wanted you to know the money is still there if you need it. I know things must be tight for you after everything that's happened. All you need to do is shout. Love D x

I show the message to Tom and he raises his eyebrows.

'What do you think?' I ask him.

'Well, he still didn't say sorry. I dunno. I don't really want to say anything, if I'm honest. It's not my place.'

'No, please,' I say. 'I want to know what you think. I won't be offended, I promise.'

'Alright. Well if you don't mind me being honest, I read that as if he's saying he knows you're going to need him eventually. It sounds a bit condescending to me. Sorry. I didn't want to say anything.'

'No,' it's fine,' I say. 'I think you're right, actually.'

I know I should see Dad's reply as supportive and fatherly, but all I can do is read between the lines and see something else. I see him telling me he doesn't think I can be independent, financially or otherwise, and that he's somehow expecting me to come running back to him. I don't need to send him a reply. There's nothing that needs saying. Actions will speak louder than words.

20

The doorbell rarely rings at this time in the morning, but it has, and it's yanked me from my sleep. My first thought is to try and remember what I must have ordered from Amazon recently. My second is that it says a lot about my life that I automatically assume the only person who'd pay me a visit at the weekend is a delivery driver.

I throw on my dressing gown and head downstairs before opening the door. The second I see Mum and Dad standing there, and before I've even registered the looks on their faces, I know exactly what's happened.

'No,' I say, my legs turning weak and my eyes fluttering as my dad steps inside and embraces me.

'Sweetheart, I'm so sorry,' he says. The man who's just lost his mother, whose first instinct is to act as a rock to everyone else.

'The carer found her in bed this morning,' Mum says.

'She'd died in her sleep. She looked very peaceful, apparently, and wasn't in any pain.'

I know this should come as some relief, but it really doesn't. Even though we'd all expected it to come at any moment, known that she didn't have long left, nothing makes it any easier.

Nan had always refused to go into hospital or into a care home, and had instead chosen to have a carer visit her at home twice a day. My parents and other family members would pop in occasionally during the day to keep her company or help her with her lunch, but the professional carers would do the morning and evening routines. It must have cost her a packet, but she was adamant and determined that she wanted to remain at home and keep that last element of independence. It'd been an admirable stance to take, and had probably kept her alive longer than going into an MRSA-infested hospital or a soulless care home would've done.

Mum takes me through to the lounge while Dad goes through to the kitchen to make us all a cup of tea.

'I'm not even dressed or showered,' I say, as if this is the sort of event everyone should be dolled up for.

'Don't worry about that,' Mum says. 'We've seen you in worse states over the years. Besides which, we didn't really feel right ringing you up and telling you we were coming over. It was the sort of thing we felt we needed to tell you in person. We wanted to be here with you.'

I smile helplessly. 'How's everyone else?' I ask,

presuming aunts, uncles and cousins will have found out by now too.

'They're okay. As well as they can be, of course. I think everyone knew it was due to come at some point soon, but it doesn't make it any less upsetting for anyone. Your uncle Tony's taken the lead and will be organising funeral arrangements. Apparently your nan had it all planned out in a notebook. She'd chosen the music, the venue, the lot. She even knew which pub she wanted the wake to be held in.

I let out a noise that's halfway between a sob and a chuckle. That was typical of Nan. Before she'd become housebound, she used to go out each afternoon to collect the shopping for the next day. She never did a weekly shop, but picked up a couple of small bits each day, making sure she came home via the same pub, where she'd pop in and order half a pint of stout before drinking it and coming back home. She credited that daily drink for her longevity, completely ignoring the fact it was probably the walking to and from the shop that helped her health, and that the beer on the way home had probably not helped in the slightest.

But that was the way she was. It was the way she'd always been, and no-one was ever going to change her. She still had her habits and her routines from decades earlier — many of them from the war — and they'd done her just fine her entire life, thankyouverymuch. She'd been the matri-arch for years, and even in her final days she'd always been keen to tell everyone exactly what was on her mind — a trait my dad has always suffered from, too. Plain talking, honest and real. No holds barred.

I wonder what she would have said to me if she'd known I'd been moping around the place worrying about petty arguments and fallings out. In fact, I don't wonder at all. I know exactly what she would have said. She would have told me to pull my socks up and stop being so ridiculous. Far less logical and analytical than Cath, but just as motivational. She would have told me it was silly to get so worked up about a man I met on the internet, and that this probably meant he wasn't a real person at all but was somehow some sort of digital hologram. She never did understand technology. In the end, we gave up trying to explain it to her. What was the point? In any case, her words of advice would have been the same. Stop being daft, man up and get on with it.

And, like Cath, she might not have been too far from the truth.

21

THURSDAY 2 JANUARY

The first day back at work after Christmas and New Year is always a slow, subdued one, but this year's even worse than most.

Even though Nan's death wasn't exactly unexpected or unforeseen, it's still hit me pretty hard. I guess there's no way you can ever really prepare yourself emotionally for something like that. Worse, you have to watch your loved one slowly decline and lose everything they once were before having to go through it all again in one fell swoop when they finally die.

Being back at work will probably help take my mind off things — at least until the funeral.

We spent New Year's Eve at home, watching the telly. I didn't feel much like celebrating, and I stopped going out for New Year years ago when it started to cost twenty quid to even get into a pub, not to mention being packed in like sardines and having to queue for three quarters of an hour to get a drink.

But hey. New year, new me, as the saying goes. It's time to get back on the horse and have a damn good go at making this year better than the last.

As I walk into the office, Sue spots me and walks over.

'Grace, can I have a word please?' she says.

This worries me. Sue and I have a very friendly relationship, and everyone in the office is casual and playful. This seems a little formal.

I follow Sue into her office and close the door behind me.

'I've had Matilda Dewitt on the phone,' she says.

'Ah. Yeah, she sent me an email. I sent a few comments to you about it just before Christmas, but I don't know if you've read them yet. It'll probably be somewhere amongst all the—'

'Yes, I've read them,' Sue says, interrupting me. 'And so has Matilda.'

My heart lurches and I feel the colour draining from my cheeks. 'Excuse me?'

'That email you sent to me, calling her out and slagging her off. You sent it to her, too.'

I struggle to catch my breath as I begin to realise the enormity of what Sue's saying.

'No I didn't,' I say. 'That's not possible.'

'Of course it is, Grace. We've all sent emails to the wrong people before. It's especially easy when you're talking about that person and end up typing their name into the wrong box. And that's exactly why it's such a bloody stupid idea to use your official company email to slag off our most important and high-paying clients.'

Sue's furious. I can see it in her eyes. Any pretences of our friendly relationship are completely gone, and I can tell this isn't going to end well. Even the most relaxed of working relationships have their boundaries, and this has well and truly breached ours.

'I... I don't know what to say. I can't even remember what the email said.'

'Maybe I can jog your memory,' Sue replies. 'How about "She turned it down because she didn't want her snooty Z-list arse-lickers to get butthurt by being demoted to the second or third round of admissions"? Or perhaps the bit where you called her a "snotty bitch"? If that's not enough, maybe it was you calling her a cow twice, or maybe the bits where you referred to her "shitty gallery" and her husband's hairpiece?'

My legs turn to jelly and I sit down on the chair next to Sue's desk.

'You won't be surprised to hear she's made an official complaint,' Sue says.

'I really don't know what to say.'

Sue perches on the edge of her desk next to me. 'What on earth possessed you to send something like that, Grace?'

I shake my head. 'I don't know. We all do it. We all talk like that to each other.'

'Yes, and we shouldn't. It's not professional. And sending it to the client herself is just completely fucking stupid. We could have pacified her, you know. When she complained about the event. I could have called her up, calmed her down, reduced her bill and kept her happy. We'd still have made a tidy profit, and we'd have been in with a chance of getting to do the launches for her other gallery.'

'I'll call her,' I say. 'I'll apologise.'

'Oh no you won't. That ship's long sailed. We've got absolutely no chance. She's made a formal complaint against you, Grace. She's refusing to pay a single penny of her bill until she's satisfied that you've gone through the proper disciplinary procedure.'

My chest hurts. My eyes sting. I want this all to end.

'Right,' I say, my voice a hoarse whisper.

'We're not sure what that is yet. I've spoken to the other directors and we think we might be able to do some damage limitation on your part by leaving a bit of time for Matilda to calm down. In the meantime, we've got to suspend you pending further investigation and discussions.'

'Suspend me?'

'It's for your own good, Grace. Trust me. If we can put a bit of time between this, we might be able to bring her back off the ledge. We've lost her business, we know that, but if we can play this right, we might just be able to save you.'

'Save me?'

'According to our company disciplinary procedure, it's

gross misconduct, Grace. Your actions have brought the company into disrepute. By rights, we should terminate your employment. I'm not going to lie, that's still on the cards. But believe me, we don't want to have to do that. We're in a lot of shit and I'm locking horns with the other directors just to try and keep hold of you. You know the difficulties we've been in this year thanks to Pelham-fucking-Saunders. Three guesses who Matilda Dewitt's given her next five gallery launches to? Just go home, take a breather and let us deal with this, okay?'

I look at Sue, my eyes filling with tears as I begin to realise I might not be quite as in control of my life as I was hoping.

22
MONDAY 6 JANUARY

I haven't had much sleep over the past few nights. I've been awake for most of them, tossing and turning, worrying about what had happened at work.

I told Tom about it as soon as he got home on Thursday, and he was shocked but supportive. He told me he was sure it would all sort itself out and that Sue would be able to talk Matilda round. I'm not so sure on that front. My main worry is that she won't be able to convince the company to keep me on. We're already looking at the strong possibility of redundancies, and I doubt someone who'd recently committed gross misconduct is going to be anywhere other than top of the list when the axe falls.

I realise how damaging my stupid mistake must have been for the company, but it could be catastrophic for me. If I lose my job I'll have nothing. I've got nothing already, so

I'll have even less. I'll lose the house, without a shadow of a doubt. Tom won't be able to cover the full mortgage. He's not even covered his own half yet. And there's no way I'll be able to walk straight into another job after having just been sacked for gross misconduct and bringing my previous employer into disrepute.

Tom keeps telling me they haven't sacked me, and that there's a good chance they might not, but I think I'm pretty certain to lose my job either way. I didn't buy Sue's talk about wanting to give them some space so she could talk the other directors and Matilda around to her way of thinking. The more I mull it over in my mind, the more I've come to the conclusion that this is their way of ensuring this is still ongoing when the time comes to announce their first round of redundancies. Then they can let me go by making me redundant, effectively firing me without having to actually have me go through the ignominy of a disciplinary procedure or having it on my record. It won't make it much easier for me to get another job, though, and in any case I reckon I'd have to find something within about a week in order to avoid defaulting on payments.

I mentioned to Tom that perhaps I should start looking for new jobs now, in an attempt to have something lined up. It seemed like a sensible idea to me, but he said I should focus on having some time to myself and getting my mind straight before rushing into anything. I'd have much more chance of being successful if I'd recharged my batteries first, he said. Best to get Nan's funeral, Cath's wedding and everything else out of the way first.

As I'm making breakfast, a text comes through to my phone from Mum.

Are you at work today? x

I sigh as I tap out my response. Ordinarily, I should be at work. But it's easier to tell a little white lie.

No, working from home today. Why's that? x

I butter my toast and sit down at the table, then another message from Mum pops up.

Just wondered if we could pop in. Mid morning maybe? x

I look at the clock on the wall. It's almost ten o'clock anyway, so they're hardly giving me much notice.

Should be fine. Give me half an hour or so to finish off what I'm doing if poss? x

Sure x, comes the reply.

I scoff breakfast, jump in the shower and try to make myself look presentable. A moment before they arrive, I flip open my laptop and bring up a couple of random spread-sheets, then spread my notebook and pen next to it, so it looks like they've caught me in the middle of something important. Might as well keep up appearances.

When they arrive, I offer them both a cup of coffee. Tom and I don't drink coffee, and we only bother with it when Mum and Dad come over. Mum tells me they're only passing through, though, so no coffee today.

'Tom at work?' Dad says.

'Yeah, he is. He's got meetings and all sorts.'

'We wanted to ask you something, actually,' Mum says, changing the subject. 'It's a little delicate, so we hope you don't mind.'

I can tell by the tone of Mum's voice and the general atmosphere that something about this is going to be pretty awkward.

'Go on,' I say.

Mum sits down at the kitchen table, and Dad leans back against the wall, his arms crossed, backside propped on top of the radiator.

'Well, we've been at your Nan's place over the past day or two. Sorting out all her things, you know. Trying to work out what's got to go where. And we were wondering... Do you remember that amethyst necklace she used to have?'

'Yeah, of course,' I say. 'She used to wear it all the time.'

'That's the one,' Mum says, nodding. 'You used to love it, ever since you were a little girl. You were the only one she ever used to take it off for.'

I smile, remembering it fondly. 'I was only talking to Tom about it just before Christmas, when we realised she didn't have long left. Strange, the things that come back to you.'

Mum looks at Dad, who returns an awkward glance.

'Yes, well, there's a bit of a problem on that front,' Mum says. 'We've searched everywhere, but we can't seem to find it.'

I narrow my eyes. 'That's weird. She wasn't wearing it when she... you know...?'

'No. She only had her wedding ring on. They itemise everything. Sordid, I know, but that's how it is. She used to take it off every night when she went to bed, but then she'd always lay it out neatly on her bedside table. We presumed that's where it would be, but it's not.'

'Oh. That's weird. Have you asked the carers?'

Mum nods. 'Yes, but they don't know anything about it. They haven't been back since she passed, of course. No-one has, other than your Dad and I. As far as we know.'

'As far as you know?' I ask. There's an odd inflection in her voice which tells me there's some sort of hidden meaning there, but I can't quite catch it.

'Well, we wondered if perhaps you'd been back there at all. To reminisce, maybe, or help... I don't know, tidy up or something.'

'No, of course I haven't. Why would I do that?'

'We don't know,' Mum replies. 'But we can't seem to think of any other explanation for it.'

Now I'm catching on. 'Hang on a second. You think I took the necklace?'

'No, no, of course we don't,' Mum says. 'I mean, you might have looked at it, or moved it or borrowed it.'

'Or Tom did,' Dad says, his first words since arriving.

I look at him and cock my head. 'Tom?'

'Well we know you wouldn't take it,' Mum says, her voice almost a conspiratorial whisper.

'And neither would Tom,' I reply, refusing to dip my own volume.

Mum looks round, as if he's going to be able to hear her, even though they know damn well he's at work.

'Perhaps it's an honest mistake, Grace. Maybe the last time you were visiting he saw it and... I don't know, perhaps he just—'

'Are you actually serious?' I say, raising my voice. 'Is this some sort of joke?'

'We can't think of any other explanation, Grace,' Dad replies.

I stand up and push my chair in, looking at them both.

'Well you're wrong,' I say. 'Tom didn't take it. And do you know how I know? Because he's never even set foot in her house, that's why. How dare you come round here and accuse him of doing that? After everything that's been said and done over the past few days!'

Mum stands up and moves towards me. 'Darling, we just—'

'No, Mum! I've had enough. Get out. Both of you. Just get out!'

They look at each other, Mum giving Dad a look that says *I told you this was a stupid idea*, before they both leave.

I didn't dare tell Tom what Mum and Dad said. I know he'd have been supportive and told me they were just under stress, didn't know him that well and had no other option, but it doesn't matter. How on earth do you tell your own partner that your parents suspect him of stealing your dead Nan's jewellery?

I really don't know what they've got against Tom. Maybe they're just hell-bent on me staying single. They were broken when Matt left and they realised it was over between us. If they ever have realised, that is. I still don't think they've come to terms with it. Part of me wonders whether they want me to be happy because there's a chance it might go wrong again. Maybe they're just waiting for Matt to come back into my life, or for me to go chasing him and asking for him back because things were so much better before.

I'm pretty sure Tom can tell something's up, but he doesn't say anything. He probably just thinks I'm still upset about Nan and the work thing.

Cath's wedding is next month, and I'm desperately hoping I'll be able to put on some sort of a brave face for it. At the moment it feels as though the whole world is crashing down on me.

While we're busily watching some rubbish on TV, Mum texts to ask if they can come over. My heart sinks. It didn't exactly go all that well the last time they did that. But she adds a caveat: she wants to apologise.

Having them over would mean telling Tom about what happened, the things they'd accused him of, and I really don't want to have to do that. But Mum's follow-up text tells me I might not have much choice.

Please. We're outside x

I daren't open the curtains and peer out, because they'll see me. Not that they don't already know I'm in here, of course. But the fact they've turned up and parked outside the house without even contacting me first *really* pisses me off.

'What is it?' Tom says, noticing something's wrong.

So I tell him. I have to. I've got no choice.

'I don't really know what to say,' he replies, calm and dignified.

'You don't need to say anything,' I tell him. 'It's ridiculous. You've never even been in Nan's house. I told them that.'

Tom sighs. 'So do they think it's you?'

'I've no idea. Probably. I don't really care. They'll find it eventually and look like a pair of idiots, then they'll have to come running back to apologise to me with their tail between their legs. Then something else will happen and that'll be my fault too. The cycle continues.'

Grace? x

I tap out a reply.

Give me five minutes.

'Maybe they've found it,' Tom says. 'Maybe that's why they've come round. To apologise.'

'In that case, you've got a higher opinion of them than I have,' I reply.

I go upstairs and get changed, then come back down and wait for the doorbell to ring. When it does, I get up and open the door. I don't say a word.

'Can we come in?' Mum says.

I stand back and let them in, then Tom comes out of the living room, friendly and courteous as ever.

'Coffee?' he says.

'No,' I reply, before they can. 'They won't be here long enough for that.'

Tom walks back into the living room looking like a scolded child, and I stand in the hallway, waiting to hear what Mum and Dad have to say.

We stand in silence for a few moments, almost as if they're expecting me to speak first — as if I have anything I want to say to them after the way they've treated me and Tom. Eventually, I walk through into the living room and sit down. My parents follow me.

As is so often the case, it's Dad who breaks the silence.

'Grace, we're well aware that things haven't really been getting off on the right foot lately.'

I make a noise that's halfway between a snort and a huff and cross my arms.

Dad continues. 'And we're also well aware that we might have jumped the gun a couple of times and not got our points across in the right way.'

'Let me stop you there,' I say, interrupting him. 'This isn't about you being misunderstood or not getting things across in the right way. You came over here while Tom was at work and you out-and-out accused him of being a liar and a thief.'

'That's not quite what we said,' Mum replies, shuffling awkwardly in her seat.

Tom, dignified as ever, says nothing and does his best not to look offended.

'Look at it from our point of view,' Dad says. 'The bloody sun's position is less predictable than that necklace's was. Then the second Mum's dead, it disappears. The only people who've been in there or who've got keys is us and you.'

'And the carers.'

'Come on, Grace. If the carers were going to nick her jewellery, they'd have done it on one of the thousand other times they were in the house. Why wait until she's dead?'

I shrug. 'So there'd be no witnesses and she couldn't say it was missing?'

'I'm not being funny, love, but a fortnight before she died she claimed Alfred the Great was living in her wardrobe. They could've nicked the roof from over her head and she wouldn't have noticed.'

'The paramedics and the doctor were in the house,' I say. 'And the police.'

'Police?' Tom asks.

'Standard procedure,' Mum says. 'It's because she died at home. They have to come out as a matter of course to rule out foul play. And a doctor has to pronounce her dead.'

'Unless you're trying to tell me it was the police who nicked her necklace,' Dad adds.

I look at him, a blank expression on my face. 'I don't know what you want me to tell you,' I reply. 'I haven't been up there since she died, and Tom's never been in his life. I don't know how you imagine we pulled off the Great Heist.

An elaborate set of magnets, perhaps? A series of homing pigeons with lock picks?'

'There's no need to get sarcastic, Grace.'

'Trust me, Dad. Sarcasm is the least of your worries right now.'

'Look,' Dad says, leaning forward. 'We're just concerned. Maybe we didn't get it right. That's fine. I'm sure there's a perfectly innocent explanation.'

'Like the care workers on minimum wage who are practically strangers and had unfettered access to her place while she was lying there dead, you mean?'

Mum and Dad share a look.

'Perhaps,' Dad says. 'I'll have a look at the CCTV from the front door around that time, but I doubt very much it'll be any use unless the thief skipped down the front drive twirling the fucking thing around in the air.'

'Looks like it's the best hope you've got,' I say. 'Because it wasn't anything to do with me or Tom. I told you. Tom's never set foot in that house.'

'In that case, Thomas, we're sorry,' Dad says. I genuinely think it's the first time I've ever heard him use those words.

'Thank you,' I say.

'Thanks,' Tom adds. 'If it's alright with you guys, I'm going to go upstairs for a bit and give you all some space.'

Mum and Dad say nothing as Tom leaves the room and jogs up the stairs to the bedroom.

'Look, maybe we were overreacting, but it does come from the best possible place, we assure you,' Mum says.

Dad seems to be either pacified by the clearing of the air or feeling awkward at the way things have played out. It's impossible to tell which. 'How are things going at work?' he says.

I swallow hard. 'Fine. Absolutely fine.'

Dad nods. 'Any interesting projects on at the moment?'

I shake my head. 'No, not really.' It's not a lie.

'And money? Are you okay for money?'

'Yes, fine thanks,' I say.

'No worries on that front at all?'

'No. None. All fine, thanks.'

Mum and Dad look at each other, then back at me.

'You know you can always come to us if you're struggling, don't you?' Mum says. 'Money-wise, I mean.'

My eyes narrow. 'But I just told you I was absolutely fine. Twice.'

'I know you did, dear. But we just want to.... check.'

'You don't believe me.'

'Of course we do. We just want to make sure.'

'How many times? Three? Four? Sixteen?'

'Grace...' Dad mumbles.

'If you're under stress,' Mum says, 'we can help you out. We've all been there. It's difficult at times. And we know you've been worried about potential redundancies at work, and... Well, if something were to happen on that front then we'd be able to help.'

There's something in the way they say this that makes me wonder. This isn't them just mentioning things on the off-chance I might bear it in mind in the future. This isn't a case of checking I'm alright. There's more to it. Almost as if they *know* something is wrong.

I force a smile. 'No. Like I say. Everything's fine, thanks.'

UNTITLED

This house is about as soundproof as a cardboard box. That's something that tends to be an inconvenience, but which I'm now grateful for.

It's always fascinating to hear what your parents have to say when they think I'm not listening. They haven't dropped me in it, though, which is handy. They haven't told you that I confided in them about the difficulties you've been having and your problems at work.

I was just looking out for you, you understand. It was only right they knew. They needed to, Grace. This way, you can prove to yourself that you can stand on your own two feet. You'll be able to tell them — and yourself — that you don't need them. I know you're ready. I know this is where you finally break free.

They won't say anything. Not directly. They assured me it would be confidential, and I persuaded them I was only looking out for your best interests. And I am. I always am. Nothing else matters but you. Us.

I can see they're trying to push you. I know you've realised. You've finally reached the point where you don't need them. I have faith in you, Grace. I know you'll back away. You don't need them. You're so much better off without them. This is the test.

I hope I didn't show a reaction when your dad mentioned the CCTV. Stupid, stupid. I can't see it being a problem, though. I had my hat pulled forward that day, just in case. You can never be too careful. Besides which, I've got plenty on my side. As you rightly told them, I didn't even know the address, did I? In a way, part of me hopes they still suspect. Because then they'll keep pushing. Pushing you away.

You can see the sort of people they are now. You know you're better off without them. I'm going to have to keep my wits about me. Keep a close eye on them. Because otherwise I'm going to have to do something about them.

It's you and me against the world.

24

I wake up with a sore head after one too many drinks the night before. We decided to head into town for a bit of a blow-out, which seemed like a good idea at the time. Tom wasn't drinking, as per usual, but I certainly had more than my fair share.

While he's still snoring away in bed, I decide to get up and do a bit of housekeeping. Once the headache's cleared a bit, I decide to brave looking at a screen and check my bank balance. I mostly used my debit card to buy drinks yesterday, and am worried about how much I might have spent.

The online banking app loads and I log in. The balance immediately looks off. By quite a bit. I don't check my balance half as often as I should do, but I'm pretty certain this isn't right.

I scroll back through the history, and nothing looks out

of place. Until it strikes me. The mortgage money's gone out, but Tom's half hasn't come in to help cover it. As a result, I'm hundreds of pounds down.

I'm sure it's an innocent mistake. I wouldn't normally mind, but after the expense of Christmas I'm already in my overdraft as it is.

Half an hour or so later, he comes plodding downstairs in his boxers and heads straight for the thermostat.

'Probably be a bit warmer if you put some clothes on,' I say. 'And it'd save us money.'

I wonder if this will prod his memory, but I'm pretty certain it won't.

'I'll get dressed after I have a shower,' he says, yawning. 'Not much point doing it twice in the space of ten minutes.'

'Well, the place is clean. Ish. Just trying to get a few things ticked off my list so I can collapse on the sofa this afternoon. I've sorted out the kitchen, tidied the living room, done the finances. Oh, that reminds me,' I say, as if it's a minor thing I'd almost forgotten. 'For some reason your half of the mortgage hasn't been coming through.'

'Oh. Yeah. Sorry about that. Problems with the bank. I'll get it sorted, I promise.'

'When?'

'I don't know. Christ, I've only just woken up.'

'I know, but it's important, Tom. I'm in the red as it is, and I don't know if I'm going to have a job for much longer.'

'Alright, I'll try and sort it out today.'

This sounds like an excuse to me. 'You've been living

here for a while now and you said you'd contribute your half.'

'Yeah, and I will. I just said I would, didn't I? I'll speak to my boss and see what I can do.'

'Your boss?'

I swear I see Tom wince slightly. 'Yeah, some sort of problem with the finance department. They haven't been paying people on time. Just an admin error apparently. Nothing to worry about, but it's slowing things down.'

'I thought it was a problem with the bank?'

'It is. Something between the finance department and the bank. I don't really know. All far too complicated for me.'

'How are you paying for things?' I ask.

Tom shrugs. 'There's not much to pay for. He's been forwarding me a bit of cash to keep things going in the meantime. It's fine, these things happen. I'm not worried, so you definitely don't need to be.'

'I am worried, though, Tom. I'm not made of money. Do you think it'll come in before the end of the month?'

'Honestly? I've no idea, babe.'

'Because if it doesn't I'm going to max out my overdraft. There'll be nothing left.'

Tom scratches his head. 'Can't you speak to your parents?'

'And say what?'

'I don't know. The truth. Tell them the finance department have fucked up at work and what with Christmas and everything you're having cashflow issues.'

'I can't do that, Tom. You know I can't. They stopped subbing me when you moved in. And I'm not going back to them after everything that's happened.'

Tom shrugs again. 'I dunno. Maybe. But there's not a whole lot we can do about it, is there?'

I watch as he trundles back up the stairs towards the bathroom, leaving me with the metaphorical mess downstairs.

25

It's the day of Nan's funeral. It isn't a day I've been looking forward to, but one I've been looking forward to getting out of the way.

It looks as if there's going to be a good turnout. Nan had made a lot of friends over the years through the church — something else which helped us ensure the funeral arrangements were sorted out quickly — and it was heartening to see so many of her friends and family from around the country, and further afield, saying they wanted to come to pay their last respects.

Tom's been incredibly supportive, too. He's spent most of the rest of the time working, keeping an eye on things from home and trying to deal with the work project from his laptop. It doesn't seem to be causing any problems, which has put me at ease.

We're due to meet the rest of the family at my parents'

in a couple of hours, and Tom's busy working on his laptop while I get ready. As I'm doing my make-up, I catch sight of the computer screen in the mirror. It looks familiar.

'I thought you said it was best for us to hide our social media profiles?' I ask him, trying to make it sound as casual and non-combative as possible.

'I did,' he says, after a short pause. 'I'm just checking on some work stuff on Facebook. I've got a dummy account for that, under a false name so I can keep an eye on things. No way around that, unfortunately.'

'What sort of stuff?'

'I can't say,' he says, shutting me down immediately.

I don't know much about the ins and outs of Tom's job — it always seems way beyond me – but I didn't think it had anything much to do with Facebook or social media.

'Is it to do with those guys who got sacked?' I ask. Maybe he's got to keep an eye on them, or perhaps he's watching what other employees are saying and doing. There are always stories online about bosses spying on their staff's social media accounts, trying to make sure they're not badmouthing the company or misusing it in any way.

'What? Oh, no. Don't worry about them. They won't be a problem.'

'Oh right. Well, that's good. Does that mean we can put our accounts back up again?'

'No,' Tom says, quickly. 'Not yet. Best to play it safe. I'll speak to my boss and see what he says.'

'Was it his decision then?'

'No. But he'll have a better idea of what it's like on the ground. I haven't been over there, so I don't want to make any decisions at the moment. I'll speak to him and let you know.'

I nod. 'Got much left to do?'

'Hopefully not.'

'We've got to leave in twenty minutes,' I say. We've agreed to pick up one of Nan's friends on the way.

'I know,' Tom says. 'I'm perfectly capable of telling the time.'

'Alright. Just saying. We don't want to be late.'

In the mirror, I see Tom whip round and glare at me. 'We're not going to be late, alright?'

'Okay,' I say. 'Fine. Sorry.'

I carry on getting ready, the silence deafening between us. Fifteen minutes later, though, I'm starting to get more and more anxious, and I now know we're almost certainly going to be late.

'Tom?' I say, poking my head around the bedroom door. 'We've got less than five minutes. We need to go.'

If I'd seen the look on his face before I started talking, I don't think I would have said anything. The anger and tension had clearly been building before I even came into the room, and now it explodes in a way I've never seen Tom react before.

'For fuck's sake, Grace! Stop fucking badgering me, alright? If you want to go, go. There's hours to go until the funeral, so what's the rush? She's fucking dead already, what's another ten minutes going to matter?'

The words hit me like a bullet, and I try to tell myself this isn't how he'd normally react. He's stressed because of work. Because of the guys he had to let go. Because he's miles away from it all, back here, having to go to a family funeral.

'Tom, please don't say things like that,' I reply, my voice almost a whisper.

'Why not? What does it matter?' he barks.

'Because we're all very upset at what's happened and today's going to be a difficult day for all of us. It's probably best if we keep calm heads.'

Tom scoffs. 'She was an old woman who was going to die anyway. What's the point in getting upset about it?'

'She was my nan and I loved her,' I say, fighting back the tears whilst doing my best to stand up to his comments. I know he doesn't mean them. He's upset too, and sometimes people react badly. This isn't him. It's not the Tom I know and love.

'Alright, fuck's sake,' he says, slamming his laptop lid shut and casting it to one side. 'Get out of my way, then. At least let me get dressed in peace.'

I swallow — hard — then head downstairs to wait for him.

26

We drove in silence to my parents' house, only making polite conversation with Nan's friend after picking her up. The atmosphere could have been cut with a knife, but as far as anyone else was concerned that was entirely down to the occasion. Funerals are rarely happy events, even at the best of times.

If truth be told, I'm waiting for Tom to apologise. It won't automatically make things better, but it'll at least tell me he recognises what he says and regrets it. Well, at the very least it'll mean he knows he's upset me.

When we get to Mum and Dad's house, the formalities kick in. There are lots of hugs, plenty of it's-been-years-since-I've-seen-yous and even a few my-haven't-you-growns. Tom works his way around, introducing himself to anyone he hasn't already met. It always amazes me how he can put on a totally different face in front of others. I guess that's what makes him such a people person.

'Listen,' he says, walking up to me while I'm in their kitchen making tea and coffee. 'I'm sorry about earlier, alright? I'm up to here with all the work stuff, and I shouldn't have snapped. I know it's no excuse, but I was in an email conversation with my boss all morning about the situation over there, and when you walked in I'd just got a message from him saying the client in China had heard about the guys we'd let go and were threatening to pull the deal.'

'Oh no,' I say, realising the enormity of the situation. 'Can they do that?'

'I don't know. That's for the legal guys to sort out. He reckons he's pacified them for now, but we're skating on really thin ice. You can imagine how it looks. They've hired us to design a state-of-the-art computer security system to keep them safe from criminals, and find out we've hired three of them to build the system. It's like hiring a bank robber to fit a new front door at NatWest. Absolute fucking shambles.'

'But it'll be alright? I mean, if you rumbled the guys and got rid of them, it should all be smooth enough from here, shouldn't it?'

Tom shrugs. 'You'd hope so, wouldn't you? But at the end of the day, if they failed to even do basic background checks on the people they were hiring, it makes you wonder what else we've missed. We might have got away with that particular fuck up, but the client will be on the look out for any little mistakes now. We've got to tread carefully.'

'Will they need you to go over there?'

'I don't know. I hope not, but who knows? I'll do my best to make sure I don't need to. Fingers crossed, eh?'

'Yeah. Fingers crossed,' I say, stirring another cup of tea.

The service goes off without a hitch, other than Dad making a remark to Mum about how they're now the oldest generation and will probably be the next to die. She wasn't too keen on that idea, being four years older than him.

It's refreshing to see so many people talking fondly of Nan and celebrating all the good she did with her life, instead of being upset that she's gone. That gives all of us a lot of comfort, although it doesn't make things any easier.

At the wake, I'm left talking to a couple of distant relatives — Stan and Vera, apparently, although I haven't the foggiest who they are — while Tom circles the room with Mum, meeting anyone he didn't get to speak to before the service. Everyone seems enraptured by him. It's plain to see why his boss likes to make sure he's out there on the ground, speaking with the clients and spurring employees on. I can easily see how that might be a huge benefit in a business situation. He must be worth his weight in gold.

Once they're done, Tom joins me and sits at the table with the Stan and Vera.

'You okay?' he asks me, rubbing my forearm.

'I think so, yeah,' I say. 'You?'

Tom purses his lips and nods. I can see tears forming at the edges of his eyelids.

'You sure?' I ask.

'I'll be okay,' he replies, sniffing and wiping his eyes. 'It's just really nice to hear so many people saying such nice things about her. She was clearly an amazing woman. I just wish I'd met her and spent time with her.'

I smile. 'She was very popular.'

'So it seems. I can see how much she meant to everyone. I can't even begin to imagine how you must all feel. Some of the stories family and friends have told me... What a woman.'

Tom forces a smile, kisses me on the forehead, and heads to the bar.

'He seems so lovely,' Vera says. 'You're very lucky to have him.'

'A proper old-fashioned gent,' Stan chimes in. 'Not many like him around anymore. You want to hang onto that one.'

As I gaze across the room at Tom, watching him work his charms on the bar staff, I think I know exactly what they mean.

'Grace,' a voice says from behind me. I turn around. It's Cath.

27

'You made it in the end,' I say, as Cath sits down next to me.

'Of course. I was at the service, too, but at the back. I had to rush off for a doctor's appointment. I thought I'd best pop back for some of the wake, too. Say hi to everyone.'

I smile at her, but something seems off. She's looking at me as if I've just fallen out of the sky.

'Is something wrong?' I ask.

'I was going to ask you the same thing.'

'Sorry, Cath, I'm not quite sure what's going on.'

'Yeah. Ditto.'

'Alright. Let's wind back a bit. You've totally lost me. Am I meant to know about some sort of issue or problem?'

'You tell me,' Cath says, shrugging and leaning back in her chair. 'I've not been able to get any sense out of you since before Christmas.'

I blink a few times, unsure quite what to say. 'Cath, I don't think I've even spoken to you since before Christmas.'

'Yeah. Exactly,' Cath replies.

'I mean, we've had a lot going on. What with Christmas itself, Nan dying, work. We quite often go a few days without talking and it's never caused an issue before.'

'No, but then again you've never deliberately ignored my messages before.'

My eyes and mouth widen. 'Sorry, what? I haven't ignored anything, Cath. I've not heard hide nor hair from you since Brighton. What am I supposed to have done?'

Cath pulls her mobile phone out of her handbag, unlocks it, taps the screen a few times then hands it to me. I can see, quite clearly, a series of messages on the screen from her to me.

'Cath, this is the first time I've seen any of those. Look,' I say, taking my own phone out and bringing up the message thread. 'I didn't receive any of those.'

'Well I sent them. You can see them here. You didn't even reply when I said Merry Christmas and Happy New Year.'

'Is that why you came here today?' I ask her. 'Because you thought I was ignoring you?'

Cath's face drops. 'No, Grace. I came here to pay my respects to your Nan and to give my best wishes to your grieving family. For fuck's sake, what is wrong with you?'

'I'm sick of being accused of things I haven't done, that's

what. I didn't get any messages, alright? Why the hell would I ignore you?'

Cath looks at me and moves her jaw a little, as if in consideration, before tapping her screen a few times, then looking back at me.

'What?' I ask.

'Has it come through?'

'Has what come through?'

'The message I just sent you. Show me.'

I sigh in disbelief, then show Cath my phone.

'See? Nothing. There's obviously some sort of problem with the phones. Now, do I get an apology or what?'

Cath glances at me out of the corner of her eye as she navigates out of my Messages app and into my phone's settings. I can't quite see what she's doing, but a few seconds later her face turns white and she moves her eyes slowly up to meet mine.

'What? What is it?' I ask.

'You blocked me,' she says, her voice almost a whisper.

'What? No I didn't. Give me that.'

I snatch my phone back and look at the screen. There, bright as day, is a full list of all the phone numbers I've ever blocked. It's just the one. It's Cath's.

28

'I didn't do this, Cath. Jesus Christ, I don't even know *how* to block a number. It's obviously some sort of mistake. Why the hell would I do that?'

Cath performs a faux shrug. 'I don't know. Because I was happy? Because I was about to get married and start the rest of my life and you were jealous?'

'Oh, come on. We spoke about that. We cleared the air. We had a great time in Brighton. Why would I *then* decide I didn't want to talk to you anymore? It's ridiculous. It doesn't make any sense at all.'

'I don't know, Grace. I said sorry to you, I really made an effort with Tom. I even invited him to the wedding, for Christ's sake. If you're still coming, that is.'

'Of course we're coming! Cath, I didn't block your number. I swear I didn't.'

I glance over at the bar, but there's no way I'm vocalising that suspicion. Cath's already conveyed her concerns about Tom, and I don't want her barking up that particular tree again.

'Maybe it's just a glitch,' I say. 'There's got to be a way of doing it accidentally. I don't even know how these things work, Cath. There's literally no reason why I'd do something like that. Think about it. It doesn't make any sense. If I'd gone to the effort of blocking your number, why would I be talking to you now, begging you to believe me?'

'Well if it wasn't you, who was it?'

'I... I don't know.'

'Because I hate to bring all this back up again, and I'm not accusing anyone of anything, but doesn't Tom work in IT security?'

'What's that meant to mean?'

'I'm just saying he'd know what to do, that's all. Like I say. Not accusing anyone of anything. Just food for thought.'

'Seriously, Cath. You're not trying to bring this up again, are you?'

Cath says nothing as Tom rejoins us at the table, having bought another round of drinks.

'Hi Cath. Didn't know you were coming today.'

Cath looks at him for a moment before smiling. 'Wouldn't have it any other way,' she says.

UNTITLED

I had sincerely hoped you weren't going to be a problem too, Cath. Grace has many foibles — we're working on those — but one of them is her forgiveness, particularly when it comes to you.

You hold a special place in her heart. I can't see why. You're lazy, ineffectual, self-centered and, quite frankly, turgid. To think that everyone else cares about your pathetic wedding, which you couldn't even be bothered to organise yourself, is the height of piteousness.

I could see the look in your eyes. You thought you'd got it all sussed, didn't you? You thought I hadn't heard, didn't know what you were talking about. It's dangerous to assume everyone else has the same level of intellect as you, particularly when you're as daft as a brush.

You weren't meant to come back. Not like this. You were meant to slowly drift away on a bed of non-communication and happily wedded bliss. I had a whole plan for the wedding day, too. Just an extra little spanner in the works to bring you crashing back down to earth, knock you down a peg or two. Now that'll have to go on the back burner.

It's not over yet, though. Far from it. If you're going to be a problem, I'm going to have to take action.

29

I placated Cath by deciding not to start an argument, but telling her I'd bear her suspicions in mind. The last thing I want is to push her away again.

With the funeral out of the way, it feels as if life is finally starting to get back to normal. We've got Cath's wedding coming up, but other than that things are starting to settle down. Until, that is, Tom drops another bombshell on me.

'I've got to go away. For work,' he says, over dinner.

'Oh. When?'

'Next Saturday. The morning after the wedding. Early.'

'Where?'

'Japan.'

'Wow. Okay. How long for?'

'Only a few days. Not long.'

I nod. 'Is this to do with the big project and the guys that got sacked?'

'No, that was China. This is a new client we've just taken on. A big one, actually. They want me to go over to meet the team. Should be a hell of a lot easier than the China one, to be honest. Fairly straightforward. It does mean I'll have to be up really early on the Saturday, though, so I won't drink at the wedding. I'll drive.'

I shouldn't, but I do feel a little disappointed at this. I'd been looking forward to us both being able to have a drink and let our hair down. Tom rarely drinks, and it's always fun to see him relaxing a little when he's got a beer or two inside him.

'Do they often tend to give you such little notice?' I ask.

'Not always. It depends on the situation, to be honest. Sometimes we know in advance. Other times they'll tell us they want us there the next day. Money talks, unfortunately. And with what these guys are paying us, if they say "jump" we ask "how high?". Just the way it is.'

'Well I hope they're paying you handsomely for it.'

'Oh yes. If all goes to plan, there'll be a nice little bonus in it for me. Then I can get caught up on the mortgage money and even give you some in advance for the next few months,' he says, almost as if he's read my mind.

'That'd be good. Things are getting pretty tight on that front.'

'I know,' he says, holding my hand. 'But we'll get through it. We always will.'

30

It's the morning of the wedding and Tom's trying to perform two jobs at once: getting dressed into his suit whilst simultaneously attempting to pack his case for his trip to Japan tomorrow.

He's got an early flight, so will be up at the crack of dawn to head to the airport. I tried to suggest we could still get a taxi to and from the wedding and he could at least have one or two drinks, but he was steadfast in his refusal.

'I don't much fancy a hangover,' he said, almost pointedly, as we discussed it a few days earlier.

Somehow, we make it on time. There aren't any official bridesmaids as such, but a few of us have been provided with matching dresses and are told to stand and look pretty in photographs. Ben's brother is the best man. I almost don't recognise him at first. I must have only met him two or three times in my life, and then only ever briefly.

Everyone is seated well ahead of time, each and every flower and order of service is perfectly crisp and aligned, and there's not even a speck of dust where it shouldn't be. Cath looks radiant in her dress as Ben waits at the front.

Once the formalities are over, we're shuffled off outside, back into the cold again, for photographs. The photographer makes a big song and dance about us trying not to look like we're freezing, telling us none of us will remember how cold it was when we're looking back at the photos. I'm pretty sure we will. I've a feeling I'll still be thawing out my toes in thirty years' time. The photos take longer than they should, because the poor photographer has to keep going inside to find people who should be in the next shot, but who've gone inside to keep warm or get drunk.

When that's all over and done with, we all head inside and congregate before the sit-down meal. By this point I've already had three drinks (Why do weddings always have to drag on like this?) and I'm desperate to get some food inside me. I've not eaten since breakfast, and we're now well beyond lunchtime.

When we finally do sit down, Ben stands straight back up again and taps his fork on the edge of his wine glass, signalling that everyone should shut up and listen.

'Firstly, thank you for coming here today to share our special day with us, everyone. I just wanted to let you all know that we know you're all hungry, so we're going to get the food out of the way first, then we'll crack on with the speeches afterwards.'

There's a loud cheer and a round of applause at this, and the best man looks a little put out that he's just been demoted to being less popular than a pork chop.

The food, when it comes, isn't great. It's better than nothing, though, and I make sure I fill myself up from the basket of bread rolls as it might be a few hours until the evening buffet is served up. Maybe they'll have bags of crisps or nuts behind the bar.

And then, once the dreadful speeches are out of the way and everyone's had enough of pity laughing, we're told to either stand up or sit down around the edge of the room so they can clear the tables ready for the evening reception.

'Alright?' Tom says, sitting down next to me on a chair at the side of the room.

'Yeah, I think so,' I reply. 'Shouldn't have had so much to drink before the food. Feeling it now.'

'You only had a couple, didn't you?'

'Three,' I say. 'Must have been the emotions and stuff, too. Big day.' Three vodkas and Cokes wouldn't normally hit me that hard. 'Oh. Plus the Prosecco and wine from the table.'

'You'll be alright. Wait for your food to get down, and you'll get a second wind for the evening bit.'

An hour later, I've had another three drinks. They seem to just keep appearing. Tom's doing his usual social bit, circling the room and talking to everyone, introducing me to a new person every fifteen minutes, having gone via the bar to get them a round of drinks and — of course — one for me too.

I politely try to join in the conversations with random work colleagues of Ben's who I've never seen before and never intend to see again, occasionally checking my watch to see when the buffet food's coming out. I need to soak up some of this alcohol.

By the time the DJ turns up and starts to play some party music, I'm feeling much brighter. I've gone past the stage of feeling tipsy and am now in full-blown party mode. It doesn't happen often, but when it does I love it.

I've just finished boogieing away to Shakira when I come over to the side of the room and hold my hands out to Tom.

'Come and dance!' I shout, over the sound of the speaker just a few feet away from us.

'I'll be alright,' he says. 'I'll sit here for a bit.'

'Come on! Don't be such a spoilsport. Everyone else is dancing. Apart from the old fogeys. Are you an old fogey?' As I say the words, a part of my brain tells me I'm being an idiot, but I quickly hush it up.

'I'll join you a bit later,' he says, standing up and talking into my ear. 'I think you've probably had a bit too much to drink.'

'You're only saying that because you're being all sober and boring.'

'Someone's got to drive us back. Plus I'm up first thing

tomorrow for my flight. Let me get you a soft drink or some-thing, yeah? You don't want to make a fool of yourself.'

I shrug, then turn and go back to the dance floor as Tom goes to the bar.

A couple of minutes later, he's signalling to me with a glass of Coke. I decide to cut my losses and head over to him.

'Get this down you,' he says. 'Might give you a fighting chance. The caffeine content will help too.'

I pick the glass up, take the straw out and down the entire drink in one. The bubbles burn my nose as I try to adjust, and a few seconds later I feel a strange kick. If I didn't know Tom better, I'd have thought that was another alcoholic drink. And not a weak one, either.

'You're stumbling around and getting some strange looks from people, Grace. Maybe it's best we get you home.'

'Don't be stupid, I'm fine. Everyone's having a good time. We're just dancing.'

'You're slurring.'

'No I'm not. I've not even drunk that much.'

'Yeah, well it seems to be affecting you. You know I don't like it when you drink too much. I've told you before.'

'Well then maybe you shouldn't have kept plying me with drinks all day and night, eh?' I say, over the thump of the music.

'I'm just trying to look after you, Grace. I'm trying to keep you happy.'

'I know,' I say. 'And I love you for it.' I lean in to plant a sloppy kiss on his forehead, but miss my mark completely. The next thing I feel is a searing pain in my elbow as I land on the floor.

31

'Tom, I said I'm sorry.'

I'm surprised by how much I need the support of the walls as I make my way into the house, and I'm now starting to feel incredibly sick.

'Yeah, well you should be. You made me look like a right twat.'

'I think it's me who looked like the twat,' I say, hiccuping as I speak and trying to hold on to my stomach. 'Tell me the truth, Tom.'

Tom turns and looks at me. 'What do you mean?'

'The drinks. They weren't just singles, were they?'

He shrugs. 'I dunno. I only bought some of them.'

'You were trying to get me drunk, weren't you?' I say, walking forward in what I think is a sultry, sexy manner. 'You were just trying to get me into bed.'

'I get you into bed every night, Grace. Now come on. Sit down and let's get some water into you.'

'Make sure it's not vodka this time, won't you? I know what you're like. Trying to get women drunk so you can take advantage of them.'

Tom's face changes. 'Grace, you're talking bollocks. Sit down now.'

'I'm fine thanks. Standing makes me less likely to be sick.'

'Yeah, and it makes you more likely to fall over. I'm trying to look after you. Now sit down.'

'Do you like looking after women, Tom?'

'Only ones I care about. Sit.'

'How many women have you cared about, Tom?'

Tom sighs. 'What are you talking about now?'

'Tell me about them. You never talk about your exes. Not even Erin.'

I notice his jaw tense. 'Why the fuck would I want to talk about them? They're in the past.'

'Your daughter isn't.'

'No. No, she isn't. But I can't start thinking about that. It's not going to do anyone any good, least of all me. Now will you sit down?'

'You should track them down, Tom. You should find them. You should find your little girl and tell her how much you love her. You should find Erin and tell her exactly what you think about her. You should tell her she's a stupid fucking bitch who shouldn't have—'

The air is thrust out of me as my back slams against the wall, Tom's hand grasped tight around my throat. His face has changed completely. He looks demonic. Unrecognisable.

'Tom, I can't breathe,' I croak, the air barely able leave my mouth. I hear the blood pounding in my ears as the edges of my vision start to turn black, and I feel my life slipping away. Inside, I'm panicking. 'Tom. Please.'

His eyes are cold, and I see something in them that I've never seen before. It's almost as if they've changed colour and he's been possessed by another being.

I feel my legs start to weaken, and my stomach lurches. Just as I'm about to finally lose consciousness, his grip weakens and I hit the floor.

I lie there for a few moments, unsure what's going on, my body adjusting back to reality. There's a piercing screech in my ears and the taste of blood in my throat. The first thing I notice is Tom's suitcase being wheeled in front of my face. As he speaks, his voice is distant, almost robotic.

'I'm going to the airport now, Grace. Goodbye.'

32

I don't know how long I lie there, but I know there's no point in chasing him. By the time I've realised what's happening, he's left the house and has probably already got his case in the car. Meanwhile, I'm left struggling for breath, barely able to stand if I do get up, and completely unable to either run or drive after him.

On top of all of that, I'm left stunned at what just happened. Part of me thinks I must have imagined it, but I know I didn't. It was too real.

He's never reacted like that before. Did I say something out of order? I try to go back over our conversation, but the exact words are out of reach. We were talking about his ex and his daughter, I remember that much. What the hell did I say to make him react like that?

Another part of me tells me it's crazy to blame it on myself in any way whatsoever. There's never an excuse for that. But it's so out of character for him. It's not normal. It's not Tom.

All of these thoughts, and plenty more, go through my mind as I slowly prop myself up on my elbows — one of them still sore from falling over at the wedding — and gradually onto my backside, before I perch on the stairs and try to recover.

My head is swimming. I'm an absolute mess. I need to do something. Am I meant to call the police now? No, that's ridiculous. I can't do that. It was just a stupid argument. I love him. I need to sober up. This is going to hurt like hell in the morning. I'm going to have one hell of a hangover. Tom won't be here. He's gone. What time is it? How can I sort this out? I need to eat something. I need to have a drink. Coffee. That's meant to sober you up, isn't it? I don't drink coffee, can't stand the stuff, but they always give people black coffee on the TV when they've had too much to drink. Black coffee on the TV. Heh. I think about pouring it all over the screen. Funny. No, not funny. There's nothing funny about this. This is crazy. You need to sober up. He just fucking *strangled* you. Walked out. He's gone. Might never come back. You need to go after him. Stupid. Can't do that. No way to do it. Won't let you in an airport now. Not now you're drunk and bleeding. Elbow's a mess. Head's a mess. Life's a mess. Need to make that coffee. That'll help.

My mobile phone pings, and I scrabble around to find

my handbag, then scrabble around a bit more to find my phone inside it. Maybe it's Tom.

It's not.

It's an email. From a name I don't recognise. Someone called Jess Caton. I don't know a Jess Caton. Normally I'd assume it was spam, but I know it's not. I know, because the subject line is *TOM RAMSAY*.

33

From: Jess Caton
To: Grace O'Sullivan
Subject: TOM RAMSAY

Dear Grace,

You probably don't know who I am. My name's Jess. I'm Tom's ex. I'm emailing you to warn you about the person Tom is. I hope I've managed to track you down before you got to find out for yourself.

To be honest, I don't know what good this email will do. If you've already found out what Tom's like, who he really is, then it's too late. If you haven't found out yet, you're probably not going to believe me when I tell you. I wouldn't have believed it either if someone had told me. But I can't sit back and do nothing. I need to warn you.

I bet he calls you Butterfly. He does that. You might not

like it — I didn't — but he still does it. There's a reason for it. I bet I can tell you some other things about your life right now. I bet you've fallen out with friends and family and aren't quite sure why. I bet something's gone wrong at work. Did you let him move in with you to get him out of 'his boss's flat'?

I bet he also told you his parents were dead. They're not. They're very much alive. I was with Tom until he moved up your way. When I started to have my suspicions about Tom, I did some digging. That's how I found out his parents are still alive. That's how I found out a lot of things about Tom Ramsay. They don't talk to him. They disowned him long ago because of the person he is and the things he's done to them. There's a reason he makes out they're dead.

I bet he told you his previous ex, Erin, left him and won't let him see his daughter. That's not true either.

I don't want to go into detail about either of those things in an email. All you need to know right now is that Tom Ramsay is a pathological liar.

I managed to get out. I was lucky. I believe there are others who haven't been so lucky, or won't be so lucky.

I don't know what I can say to make you believe me. Please, Grace, look deep inside your soul and ask yourself if you think Tom is the perfect gentleman he makes himself out to be. If you have even the slightest shred of doubt, GET OUT. He is dangerous.

You probably think I'm a psychopath or deranged. That couldn't be further from the truth. I'm a police officer with

Devon and Cornwall Police. I'm based in Bodmin. My collar number is 19442. You can look me up and see I'm real and credible.

If you're not ready to do anything yet, that's fine. I completely understand. But please, PLEASE keep this at the forefront of your mind. Keep thinking about it and asking yourself if Tom is the person you think he is, or if I might just be right.

You need to know the truth. Because otherwise it could cost you your life.

Jess x

34

I read Jess's email a second time, and I immediately feel as if I've sobered up.

Tom never mentioned an ex called Jess. He's mentioned Erin, the one who disappeared with their daughter, but even then I got the distinct impression it wasn't something he wanted to go into detail about. Understandably so. But Jess? I've never heard of her.

If what she's saying is true — *if* — then that would explain why. He's hardly going to admit to that, is he? But at the same time that doesn't make it true. Otherwise there'd be people popping up all over the place saying 'Did you know Person X is a murderer/paedophile/morris dancer?' and people would be leaving their partners left, right and centre.

Although I thought the email had sobered me up, it's becoming clear it didn't. I am, however, lucid enough to ask myself if I would have reacted in the same way to this email if I'd received it a few weeks ago. Hell, even a few days or even hours ago. It's arrived on the same night that Tom put his hands around my throat and nearly choked me before walking out of our home. Is that all part of the plan? But what plan? The more I think about things, the more complicated it gets.

I read Jess's email again, trying to take in every word, every letter, trying to make sense of it all. Why would he lie about his parents being dead? Does he not get on with them? Surely it'd be easier to just say that.

At any other time, I'd think Jess was a nutter. But so much seems to ring true. The mention of him calling me Butterfly, for starters. But that's something anyone could know. Someone in the street could have overheard that. And yes, he did tell me his parents were dead. That's also perfectly reasonable for someone else to know. If, for example, they *are* dead. Saying they're not doesn't make them alive.

She said she doesn't want to go into detail about stuff in an email. Well, of course she doesn't. But she's perfectly willing to email a stranger out of the blue and tell her that Tom's some sort of psychopath? And I'm meant to just believe her?

I mark the email as unread, then walk back out into my hallway and check the door is fully locked. Then, just for good measure, I put the security chain across. I know logically that's not going to stop anyone, but every little helps, and it makes me feel better.

I realise that by now my instinct should have been to bring this up with Tom. But even if he was right here in this house with me I still don't think I would. And why? That's the thing that keeps me wondering, makes me think perhaps there's something at the back of my mind which somehow rings true, which doesn't make Jess Caton sound like a bunny boiler but actually gives her a lot of credibility.

As I think about all this, I start to feel nauseous. It's been a day with a huge amount of emotion, an even larger amount of alcohol and now this. I don't know what to feel. I don't know what to think. But with Tom out of the house and me having to spend the night on my own, I'm also well aware that I don't need to think or feel anything right now.

The aftereffects of the alcohol and adrenaline are hitting me hard. I crawl up the stairs and into my bedroom, before climbing up onto the cold duvet and sinking my head into the pillow. I shouldn't have done this. I should get up and brush my teeth, at least, or change into something a little more comfortable. But I am comfortable. I'm...

35

The first thing I register as I wake up is the disgusting taste in my mouth. I can only imagine this is what it must be like to lick a badger's arse.

The second is the indescribable throbbing — banging — of my head. It pierces through my skull and down the back of my neck like nothing I've ever felt before. There's absolutely no way in hell those vodkas and Cokes were singles. They must have at least been doubles, if not triples. But Tom said he—

Tom. My eyes fly open as I remember last night. The fight. He left. I roll my head to the side, wincing as I do so, to see Tom's side of the bed is empty. It hasn't been slept in.

Some bits are as clear as day, and others are hazy. We got home. I was being flirty, he pinned me up against the wall, he walked out, I made coffee... Did I? No.

The email.

My heart lurches as I remember it — snippets of it. I remember feeling like it had sobered me up, but that was clearly just an illusion. I don't even think I'm sober now. I reckon I'm probably still drunk.

I reach for my phone, unlock it and notice a message on my screen.

It's from Tom.

Boarding flight now. Sorry about last night. I just wanted to make sure you were okay. I'll call you when I get to Japan x

I can deal with that later. Not much point replying back now, as he won't see it for hours.

I open my email app to read it again. A few bits have come in overnight: some spam, Tinder asking me where I've been for the past couple of months, a notification that my credit card bill is available to view online. I scroll down to find the email that came in last night. I can still remember her name. Jess Caton.

But I can't find it.

I won't have deleted it. That would've been stupid. I check my Deleted Items folder just in case, but it's not there either.

This is ridiculous. I force myself out of bed, feeling my stomach lurch as I do so, and make my way downstairs. When I get into the kitchen, I open my laptop in its position on the table, blinking at the bright glare of the screen, and enter my password. It takes me a couple of attempts to do so with my shaking hands, but I'm finally in. I open my inbox and look for Jess Caton's email.

But it's gone.

36

I *know* I received it. I read it. I can still remember bits of it. Vividly, in fact. I'm absolutely certain about it. There's no way in hell I dreamt it or imagined it. It was far too real. The whole evening was. My neck is still bruised. My elbow is still bloody. My head is still pounding with the force of a million volts. Everything is as clear as it could be, considering the circumstances, and this is no different.

There's no way I would have deleted it. Not a chance. It was something I *knew* I needed to read with fresh eyes in the morning. I even remember double-checking I'd locked the doors and put the chain across. It scared the living shit out of me. I didn't imagine it.

Yesterday is a bizarre mix of blurred memories and absolute clarity. I can still see the look in Cath's eyes as she said 'I do' to Ben. I can hear them being pronounced man and wife. But I'm buggered if I can remember what happened after that, or how we even got home. I can remember in vivid detail what happened when we got home, though.

Those big moments, those adrenaline surges, are clear as day. There's no way I imagined them. Not any of them. However, Tom's text...

Boarding flight now. Sorry about last night. I just wanted to make sure you were okay. I'll call you when I get to Japan x

It's vague. *Sorry about last night?* That could mean anything. Especially when it's followed up with *I just wanted to make sure you were okay.* How is throttling me until I almost lose consciousness making sure I'm okay? But I didn't imagine that. I can't have done.

Even though my head is ringing and my stomach is lurching, I head back upstairs and make my way to the bathroom. I take a good slug of mouthwash, which I swill around my mouth and spit out into the sink. That'll do for now. Then I look up into the mirror.

Sure as anything, there are marks around my neck. And they look like finger marks. To be fair, most of my face and neck looks red and blotchy after yesterday's events, but there's no mistaking those particular marks. I wasn't dreaming. I didn't imagine it. So Tom's text *was* dismissive. It did try to downplay the fact that he'd tried to kill me just a few hours earlier.

And that means the email might have been right. I

remember it just as vividly as I do Tom strangling me. I can still remember snippets of it word for word. *Devon and Cornwall Police. I bet he calls you Butterfly. GET OUT. Jess Caton.*

I go back into my bedroom and grab my phone. Then I pause. No. If that email has disappeared, it's because someone deleted it. Someone has access to my phone. I can't risk storing anything sensitive on there.

I turn and head down the stairs, my head pounding as I try to hold onto the contents of my stomach. When I get to the bottom, I double-check the door. It's still fully locked and the chain is across. In the kitchen, I grab the notepad and pen from the work surface and scribble down the words *Jess Caton*. I can remember them now, but I don't want to ever forget that name. Just for good measure, I write it down on two more pieces of paper, then I hide one underneath the TV stand and another behind the toilet cistern in the bathroom. I keep the third one with me. I don't know why, but I'm not taking any risks. I need to remember that name, need to be able to get to it in the future.

It feels as if I'm going mad. Twenty-four hours ago everything was normal. At least, I thought it was. And now this. All because of two events: Tom's reaction and Jess's email. What was Tom even reacting to? I try to think back, to work out why he might have responded in that way, but there's nothing there. I can't remember.

I didn't dream it, though. The marks are on my neck. At least, I presume that's what it was. It can't have been because of anything else, can it? Tom said he was only trying to make sure I was okay. What did he mean by that? Have I got this wrong somehow? Did something else happen and Tom was just trying to protect me? I don't normally forget things. Except the email to Matilda, of course. But that was only a silly mistake. Just a slip of my finger.

I go back into my kitchen and open my work laptop on the table, bring up my Outlook email software and search my Sent Items folder for Matilda's name. And that's when I see it. I didn't accidentally send the email to Matilda instead of Sue. Nor did I copy Matilda in on the email. I forwarded it on to her a full three hours after sending it to Sue.

I don't remember this. I don't recall any of it. Why would I wait three hours, then forward the email on to the person I was talking about? I try to think back to that day, remember what I was doing. Did I go out? Did I drink? Could I have done it by mistake somehow? I can't see how I could have possibly gone into my Sent Items folder, opened the email, hit Forward, typed Matilda's address in and then hit Send, all by accident. It doesn't fit. There's one option which does fit, but I can't go there. There must be a better explanation. I don't want to think of the alternative.

I look up and see the coffee jar on the work surface, next to the kettle, teabags and sugar. It's been pulled out, as if I was in the middle of making a cup of coffee. I don't drink coffee, though. I've only got that jar there for when

Mum and Dad come round, and because it came as a matching set of three with the tea and sugar ones. Then I remember. I *was* going to make a coffee last night. I thought it would sober me up. The thought of coffee now makes me feel sick. I need something though, and I think it's going to have to be a mug of tea and some ibuprofen.

I get up, walk over to the side and pull out the jar of teabags. As I'm taking the lid off, my wrist knocks the coffee jar. I go to grab it with my spare hand, and send it skittering across the surface, before it sails off the edge and smashes on the tile floor.

I close my eyes and take a deep breath. This day is not getting any better. There's ceramic shards and coffee everywhere, and I daren't even take a step back in case I get glass embedded in my foot.

I look down at the mess on the floor, the coffee granules having coated the entire kitchen floor. They're under the fridge, under the washing machine, everywhere. The shattered red ceramic stands out boldly against the scattered coffee granules, the creamy white insides of the china now visible for the first time. And that's when my eye is caught by something sparkling, glittering amongst the mess.

I bend down to get a closer look, and I notice something purple in there too. My eyes widen as I realise what it is. There's no mistaking it. It's an amethyst necklace.

37

By now I'm shaking. There's absolutely no doubt this is Nan's missing necklace. I'd recognise it anywhere. But how the hell did it end up in my coffee jar?

The immediate assumption is it must have been Tom. Just like Mum and Dad suspected. But he's never been to Nan's house. He doesn't even know where she lived. So there's no way it could have been him. It can't have been Mum and Dad, because they wouldn't have taken it and hidden it there. In any case, it's only me who uses the coffee pot when they come over. And they were the ones asking me where it had gone. They seemed really upset about it.

It makes no sense. Something isn't right. Things aren't adding up. Everything seems to be falling away from me. Just when I thought it was going perfectly, the dominoes are starting to topple. Everything is crashing down around me, and I don't know why.

Did I go to Nan's house? Yes, quite a few times. I was there a few days before she died. But there's no way she wouldn't have noticed it missing if it had been taken at that point. Her dementia hadn't got to that point, had it? I didn't notice that it had. And anyway, there's no way I'd have taken it and then forgotten about it, is there? But there's the haziness over what happened last night. The email to Matilda. Cath's blocked number. The email from Tom's ex. All of those incidents are frightening the life out of me. Why are there bits I can't remember? Why do I have blanks? Why can't I find that email now?

I take the piece of paper out of my pocket and look at it again. *Jess Caton.* Her words coming flooding back to me again. And that's when I remember the other bit: *Devon and Cornwall Police.* This is something to do with Tom. It's somehow connected with his life in Cornwall. His life before me. There's something there, and I need to know what it is. And there's only one way I'm going to be able to find out.

38

I don't take the time to think about it or plan ahead. I know where I need to be, and I know what I need to do. I pack my travel case, then gather everything by the front door. I only take the essentials. I don't know how long I'm going to be. I don't know how long it's going to take, either, but that's irrelevant right now. Tom's away, I'm suspended from work and I need to know the truth.

I load everything into my car, then go back into the house to be sick into the toilet. It clears my nausea temporarily — just enough to keep me comfortable for a while. I wonder if it'll make me any safer to drive, but I doubt it. I'll just have to be careful. I need to get away from here as quickly as possible and get to Cornwall. I don't know how long it's going to take me to discover the truth, but Tom's back in a few days, and two of those are going to be taken up by the drive down to the south west.

It's only once I'm in the car that I realise I don't know what I'm going to do down there. My first aim has to be to find Jess Caton. I'm pretty sure she said she was based in either Bodmin or Boscastle. Or was it Bideford? I think that might even be in Devon.

I look at Google Maps on my phone, trying to remember which town Jess said she worked in, but I can't narrow it down any further. Bideford definitely appears to be in North Devon, but that's still entirely possible because she works for Devon and Cornwall Police. I look at directions to Bideford, and it's showing four and a half hours at the moment. Boscastle and Bodmin are both nearer five hours, so I decide I'm heading for Bideford first. At least I'll be a hell of a lot closer than I am now.

I set off, checking to see how much fuel I've got in the car. Three quarters of a tank. I'll probably have to fill up at some point, but there'll be a motorway service station I can use. The main thing now is to get away from here and get some miles under my belt so I'm closer to Cornwall. Closer to the truth. Closer to finding out who Tom really is.

I'm only a few minutes into the journey before I start to feel sick again. The movement of the car isn't helping, but I know I'll be on the motorway soon, and that'll make things a little easier. As long as I stop thinking about how ill I feel, I'm sure I'll be okay.

On the motorway, I notice every single sign for services and ask myself if I need to stop or if I think I can make it to the next one. Each time, I drive past, sure I can make it another few miles down the road. Before I know it, the miles are dropping off and the time is ticking down to my arrival in Bideford.

Once I'm there, I'll find the police station and I'll ask for Jess Caton. I know there's a good chance she doesn't work there and she's at Barnstaple or Bude or Budleigh Salterton, but at least they'll be able to tell me which station I need to be at. I hope she's working today, too. I doubt very much they'll tell me where she lives — a complete stranger turning up and demanding to see a specific officer. I hope they'll at least get a message to her that I'm there. She'd definitely respond to that. And what if they ask me what I want to see her for? I can't say 'Because she sent me an email telling me her ex is a psycho'. I'll need to make something up. Say it's confidential. Will they fall for that? Surely everything is confidential when it comes to the police, so that won't wash as an excuse. I can't say I'm a friend of hers, when it's clear I don't even know which police station she works at.

I'll think of something. I have to. I need to. Because it's the only way I'm going to get closer to discovering the truth about Tom, one way or the other.

39

It's mid-afternoon by the time I arrive in Bideford. Apart from a quick stop at Chieveley Services to go to the loo, reset my nausea clock and fill my car up with petrol, I do the entire drive in one go.

I pass Barnstaple on my way in and wonder if I should stop there first, just in case that's where Jess works, but my sat-nav tells me it's only about ten miles and twenty minutes on to Bideford, so I stick with my original plan.

As I arrive in Bideford, the road takes me over a bridge that crosses a river, and I park up in a car park just the other side. I open Google Maps on my phone and look for Bideford Police Station. I'm really close. Zero point two miles away, apparently. But I've got a parking space and I need to stretch my legs, so I get out of the car, buy a parking ticket and walk the rest of the way.

The journey takes me back towards the bridge, then

along the waterfront for a hundred yards or so. It's beautiful, even at this time of year, and I can just imagine how the summer sun must bounce off the whitewashed buildings. The water seems to open up to a beach on the other side. This must be an estuary.

As I pass a long, high slate and stone wall, I notice a sign saying POLICE. There's a railing along the top of the wall and a building beyond that. That must be the station. I walk along a little further, and the wall starts to get shorter and shorter until it meets the road I'm walking along. I walk up the long ramp, back in the direction I've just come from, and into the police station.

By this point, I've already decided what my plan of attack is going to be. I can't imagine I look as if I'm in a great state, and I hope I can use that to my advantage.

When I walk inside, the place appears to be empty apart from one officer behind the inquiry desk. I walk up and ask to speak with Jess Caton.

'Caton?' the man says. 'Sorry, don't know that name. Does she work here?'

'I'm not sure,' I answer. 'I was told I need to speak with her and that she was with Devon and Cornwall Police.'

The man looks at me for a moment, then types something into his computer.

'She's not based at this station I'm afraid, love,' he says. 'Would you like me to pass on a message or fetch you another officer?'

'No. I really need to speak to her. Which station is she based at?'

He looks at me again, this time taking in my full appearance. 'She's at Bodmin,' he says. 'You're quite a way off patch. Would you like me to get a message to her? Wouldn't want you to drive all that way for nothing.'

'It won't be for nothing,' I say. 'How far is it?'

The police officer makes a noise like a plumber about to tell me my boiler needs replacing. 'You're looking at an hour, hour and a half. It's in Cornwall, love. If you're going to do it, I'd avoid the Atlantic Highway. A30's probably your best bet, but that can be a pig sometimes too.'

'Thanks,' I reply. 'Is she working today?'

The man lets out a small laugh. 'I'm afraid I wouldn't be able to tell you that, even if it was something I could find out on this old heap of rubbish. Which it isn't. I'll tell you what, leave your name and number with me and I'll see if I can get it to her. If she's about, I'll ask her to call you.'

I nod, then tell him my name and number. I know that if that gets to Jess, she'll be in touch. She seemed very keen to tell me all she knew. If I remember rightly, she even told me her badge number, although I've got no chance of recalling what it was. All I can do is wait for her call. In the meantime, I'm heading for Bodmin.

40

It's nearer an hour and a half by the time I get to Bodmin, and I park up in a supermarket car park just across the way from the police station. It looks more like an office block, and is situated right on the outskirts of town near a bypass, and I soon realise this isn't just a police station. It's a hub. Jess Caton must be office-based. A detective.

My heart is thudding in my chest as I walk towards the building. It's nearly quarter-to-five. Not that most police officers will work nine-to-five, of course.

What am I going to say when I get there? I was going to use the same line I used in Bideford, but the appearance of this place has thrown me completely off kilter. Bideford Police Station was an unassuming brick building at the edge of the water in the centre of town; Bodmin is a glass office block in the middle of nowhere.

My legs feel like jelly as I walk inside. The one person

who can tell me the truth about Tom could be in here. The woman who called herself his ex. Another woman who's known Tom, been with Tom. Who claims to know more about him than I do.

I go up to the front desk inside the plush building and ask to speak to Jess Caton.

'Do you have an appointment?' the young woman asks me.

'Uh, no. But I was told I needed to come here to speak to her.'

'Okay, can I take a few details?'

I decide to give her the important bits before she asks for anything awkward. 'Yes, my name's Grace O'Sullivan. The officer at Bideford Police Station said I needed to come here to speak to Jess Caton.' Not technically a lie. 'He said he'd give her a call with my details too, so she should be expecting me.'

'Okay, just a moment,' she says, picking up her phone.

As she does so, my own phone starts vibrating in my pocket. It's a withheld number. I glance at my watch, and realise the time. Could it be Tom? Has he landed in Japan yet? He said he'd ring me as soon as he had. He wasn't meant to arrive until the evening our time. I answer the call.

'Is that Grace?' the voice says. It's a woman. I know exactly who it is. And she doesn't seem at all surprised to hear from me.

'Yeah,' I say, my voice weak.

'It's Jess Caton. Listen, can you meet me in an hour?'

41

I tell the woman behind the desk not to worry, and that Jess has been in touch. I thank her, and head back to my car.

My heart's pounding and I feel sick again. The officer from Bideford must have managed to get a message to Jess. She wants to meet me at six o'clock in a pub called The Garland Ox. I look it up on my phone and see it's in the centre of town.

There's a Premier Inn a mile or so away from here which apparently has availability. It's a twenty-five minute walk from the pub. It won't leave me much time to check in and have a shower for the first time since yesterday morning, so I pull out of the car park and head for the hotel.

When I arrive, I check in and head straight for my room. The shower is hot and soothing, and I start to feel the first signs of my hangover clearing. I stay under the water for as long as I can — which is only about five minutes —

before drying myself off and getting changed. A couple of minutes after half-past five, I'm as ready as I'll ever be, and I leave the hotel and walk in the direction of the town centre.

It's cold out, and I wish I'd brought some warmer clothes with me, but there's not much I can do about that now. The cold will help clear the rest of the hangover. In any case, I've got other things on my mind right now.

I don't know what I want to ask Jess. I don't know if I want to ask her anything. I need to hear what she has to say. She claims to have more she couldn't tell me in an email. My heart jumps as I try to imagine what it might be, whether I'll believe it. Twenty-four hours ago, I'd never heard of this woman. Now I've driven to the other end of the country to find out what she's got against Tom. But I need to hear it.

The Garland Ox is a small pub on a busy street. I step inside, realising I don't even know what Jess looks like. I can only imagine I'll stand out like a sore thumb, though, and that she'll be able to spot me a mile off.

I order a lemonade and sit down at a small table by the window, and watch as people slowly file past on their way home from work or just out walking the dog. A couple of minutes later, the door opens and a woman walks in. My heart lurches as I see her. She looks almost identical to me. Her hair, face, body shape. We could almost have been twins.

She sees me and walks straight over to me.

'Grace?' she says.

I nod. 'Hi,' I say, standing and shaking her hand.

'I thought I'd recognise you. Tom's certainly got a type, hasn't he?'

'So it seems.'

Jess gets herself a drink, then comes and sits down opposite me.

'I hope I didn't shock you with that email,' she says, 'but when I found out he had a new partner I had to warn you. I totally get it if you don't believe me, or if you think I'm some sort of nutter. But I'm guessing that you probably don't, seeing as you're here.'

'Yeah. I don't really know why that is,' I say. 'Well, I do. Normally, I probably would have emailed you back or phoned you. But I read your email last night, and when I woke up this morning it was gone. I remembered your name, though, and that you said you were a police officer here.'

Jess's eyes narrow. 'Does he know you're here?'

'No. He's in Japan. For work.'

'Okay. Switch your mobile off.'

'What? Why?'

'So he doesn't know where you are. He's clever, Grace. Too clever. That email didn't just delete itself. I bet you any money Tom did it. That's what he does. He'll be able to access your emails remotely. Probably your messages and phone calls, too. And he'll almost certainly be able to see where your phone is. You need to switch it off so he can't track you any further. He'll probably already know you're here and that I've called you, but there's not a lot we can do about that. We definitely don't want him to narrow it down any further. When's he due back in the country?'

'Not for another few days. He's not even landed in Japan yet.'

Jess nods slowly and lets out a deep breath. 'Okay, good. That's a long flight. He won't have been able to track your movements today if he was on a plane himself. If you turn it off now, the last time your location will have reported back to him will have been before he switched his own phone off to get on the plane. I mean...'

'What?' I ask.

Jess's face has changed.

'That's if he did get on the plane.'

42

'Let's think this through,' Jess says. 'Talk me through it. When did he leave? When did you see the email?'

'I saw it as soon as it came through,' I said. 'Tom had already gone. He left for the airport last night. We had a bit of an argument.'

'Can I ask what about?'

I shrug. 'I don't even know myself. I was blind drunk. We were at my best friend's wedding. I marked the email as unread as soon as I'd read it, so I wouldn't miss it in the morning. As far as he's aware, I passed out drunk and never saw it.'

'Okay, good. That's good. If he thinks he's got there before you, we should be safe.'

'He's going to know something's wrong when he can't get hold of me, though. If my phone's off, he'll twig.'

'He'll know your phone's off, yeah. But if you two had a bust up last night, that'll explain it. Especially if he's expecting you to be sleeping off a raging hangover today. In any case, there's not a whole lot he can do from Japan.'

I see what she's saying, but there's something telling me I shouldn't be so sure.

'Christ, I wish I knew where to start,' Jess says. 'Basically, Tom and I met on a dating app. He knew what I did for a living, but I think he saw that as a challenge. People like Tom get a kick out of things like that. The problem for him was that I've got quite a strong personality, so he didn't get away with it. He tried to get me to come off social media, told me it wasn't a good idea with my job. But we're trained on things like that. He gave me the sob story about Erin and tried to weasel his way into moving in with me. Told me he was sofa surfing and living in some place his boss had put him up in. But I wasn't falling for any of it.'

As Jess speaks, I feel so foolish. It's the exact same story, except I fell for every single piece of it.

'Then one day he tried getting physical. He'd asked me again about moving in with me and I said I didn't want to. He flew into a rage and I told him to fuck off out of my house. I said I'd warned colleagues about him and if anything happened he'd be banged up. He hadn't done anything illegal, but I told him if I ever saw his face or heard from him again I'd make sure he went down. He did get back in touch a few days later. He was waiting for me when

I came out of the supermarket. But by then I'd done some digging at work and found out a few things about him. When I told him what I'd discovered, he went as white as a sheet. I told him to fuck off out of Bodmin, out of Cornwall and never to come back, or I'd make sure everyone knew exactly who he was and what he'd done.'

I realise I'm holding my breath, anticipating what's going to come next. I don't want to hear it, but I know I need to.

'Tell me,' I say, my voice almost a whisper.

'Look, I'm meant to be able to spot this stuff in people. It's my job. Because of that, I presumed I was safe. I mean, who'd try this sort of shit with a detective? But he'd been trying to alienate me from my friends and family, causing money issues. I had letters and emails go missing. Same as you.'

'Tell me who he is. What he's done.'

Jess takes a deep breath, then lets it out. 'He told you his parents were dead, yes?'

I nod.

'They're not. They're alive. They live locally. Down towards Polperro. He had a falling out with them years ago. Didn't have a great childhood, apparently. They couldn't pin him down and he just went off the rails. Blamed them for it. Then he meets Erin.'

Jess stops talking for a moment and seems to be trying to compose herself.

'What happened with Erin?' I ask.

Jess looks out of the window and shakes her head slowly. It looks like she's trying not to cry.

'She didn't leave him, Grace. She didn't take their daughter away. They died.'

43

I don't know what I should be feeling, and I certainly don't know what I do feel. My immediate instinct is to feel sorry for Tom, for the man I love. But I know there's more to it than meets the eye.

'What happened?' I ask.

'According to what I could find out, it was a car accident. A hit and run. Tom had been in the pub drinking all afternoon and had rung Erin for a lift home. She'd put the baby in the car and they'd driven out to collect him. They were on a road just outside town when it happened. Their car was found in a ravine. They were both pronounced dead at the scene. They found the other car later that night, but it had been burnt out. The driver was never found.'

'When?' I ask. But I think I already know the answer.

'A couple of years back. The same time he claims they

walked out and left him. The same time he says his parents died in a car accident. His parents didn't die, Grace. Erin and the baby did. Tom couldn't process that, so he twisted it in his mind. He couldn't bear the thought that they'd just been taken from him in such a totally random and unexplainable way. Maybe he felt guilty that they'd only been on that road that night because of him, because they were picking him up because he'd gone out and got blind drunk again. In his mind, he twisted it so that never happened. They'd just walked out on him and left him. All of a sudden *he* was the victim. And he got to explain his parents away at the same time. If there were any two people he wanted to die in a horrible accident, it was them. He invented a whole new reality. One that suited him.'

I feel my breathing start to get more and more shallow as my heart begins to race.

'I... I don't understand.'

'Neither did I. Not for a long time. But the more and more I look into it, the more it makes sense. Don't forget, it's my job to deal with things like this. I see disturbed people all the time. People who live in alternate realities because they can't handle the true one.'

This is too much. Too much to take in. Too much to believe. Twenty-four hours ago, everything was normal. Everyone was happy. Now I'm in Cornwall, speaking to someone who's trying to tell me Tom is some sort of lying psychopath, while he's on the other side of the world, a couple of hours away from thinking I've dropped off the face of the earth.

'I'm not sure,' I tell her. 'I need time.'

'You might not have time,' Jess says. 'Listen, you came here for a reason. You didn't hang around. You knew when you woke up this morning that something wasn't right. You didn't sit on it. You drove straight down here and went to a lot of effort to track me down. Deep down, you know the truth. Trust your gut, Grace. The alternative really doesn't bear thinking about.

Trust your gut. She's starting to sound like Tom. Telling me to stand on my own two feet. Do what I feel is right. Stop listening to others. But I have to. This time I have to listen to others. I know I need to listen to Jess.

'Grace, think about it. I know the things I've told you have rung a lot of bells. Calling you Butterfly. Taking you off social media.'

'How do you know about that?' I ask her.

'That's how I tried to find you first of all. I thought it was a bit weird you had no social media presence at all. And when I told you about Tom trying to get me to come off social media, your face dropped. Then I knew he'd done the same to you, too.'

'How did you find me? In the end, I mean.'

'I googled your name and saw that you worked for the events company. There was an old, archived LinkedIn page. I looked on the company's website and found your picture and email address. I knew you'd look just like me. Like her.'

'Her?'

'Erin. I was only half joking earlier when I said Tom has a type. That's not the full truth. The truth is he doesn't just want a woman to look like Erin. He wants them to *be* her.'

44

'Butterfly was the name he gave to Erin,' Jess tells me. 'I've been doing a lot of digging on Tom. I've spoken to his old friends. His family. I know I should leave well alone, but I needed to know. I needed to uncover everything, so I could warn people whose life he comes into.'

This all sounds weird to me. Obsessive, almost. 'Why not just use your job? Have him arrested?'

'There's no evidence of any illegal activity. He's very clever.'

'What about this?' I say, unzipping my coat to show her the marks on my neck.

'Was that him?' She asks. I nod. 'We can log that for you if you want. But I doubt it'll do much good. It'll be your word against his, and it's extremely unlikely anything will be done about it. Even if it is, he'll get off with a warning and a free pass to do whatever he wants to you. And I seriously, honestly dread to think what that could be, Grace. Don't forget this is a man who doesn't have a stable grip on reality. He's willing to lie, cheat and live a false double life in order to get what he wants. He'll go to whatever lengths it takes to keep the truth a secret. He's quite literally built his whole life around it. I'm pretty sure the only reason I managed to get out and scare him off is because of my job. He knew he had too much to lose and had bitten off more than he could chew. At first, he must have seen me as a challenge. Turns out it was a challenge that was beyond him.'

My head is all over the place. 'Okay,' I say. 'Let's assume for one minute I believe all this. I mean, I don't want to. But if I do. What now? I can't scare him off like you did. And what if he comes back? Surely now that two of us know the truth, if he is what you say he is, isn't that too much for him to risk?'

'I'm not going to lie to you, Grace,' Jess replies, her voice lowered. 'That's a very real risk. And it's one I'm deeply worried about. That's why I needed to get in touch with you. It's why I used your work email address. I presumed that would be safe from him.'

We share a look, and it's one I don't like. One which tells me absolutely nothing on this planet is safe from Tom Ramsay.

'What, then?' I ask. 'If the police can't do anything and I can't do anything, what am I supposed to do?'

Jess stays silent for a few moments, and I can see she hadn't quite thought this far ahead.

'I've got an idea,' she says, eventually. 'If he's tracking your location, he'll be doing that using some software installed on the handset. We need to get you a new handset and put your SIM card in it. Then you'll still be able to contact him and confirm he's in Japan. That'll buy us a few days.'

'And how do I explain that? If he suddenly can't track me, won't it look suspicious?'

'No. Tell him you lost your phone or it got stolen. That'd explain it going offline for a while and could even help cover your tracks if he does manage to see it's been on the move. It's not perfect, but it's all we've got.'

I look at her and see something in her eyes. I know she's telling me the truth. I don't want to believe her. I want her to be wrong. I want Tom to be the loving, caring man I know. But there's too much. It's overwhelming. And after what happened last night, I *know* there's another side to Tom. And I know I need to act fast.

45

SUNDAY 16 FEBRUARY

After our chat last night, Jess and I headed from the pub to a supermarket to pick up a cheap smartphone. I managed to get a cheap Android handset for £50. None of the numbers were saved on my SIM card, and I couldn't risk turning on my own phone, but Jess came up with the ingenious idea of installing Tinder on the new phone so I could access my old messages and get Tom's number that way.

I sent him a message as soon as I had it, telling him my phone had been stolen but that I was alright and was having to use an old handset until I managed to sort a replacement. He phoned me straight away, but I didn't answer the call. I waited until it stopped ringing, then called him back — Jess's idea — so I could hear if the phone made an international connection tone. It did. He was telling the truth about being out of the country, at least. That buys me a few days.

He sounded so normal on the phone. As if nothing had happened. I tried to sound as normal as possible, but I reckon I probably failed. Still, he'd have been expecting me to sound a little off with him after what happened last night. Plus there's the hangover. I reckon I'll have had a bit of leeway in that regard.

For now, I need to keep up the pretence that everything's normal. That means I need to be at home.

I was awake all night, trying to work out the best course of action. My heart says the best way to move forward is to wait for Tom to get back from Japan, then let him down gently and tell him I don't think it's working out. At this stage I'd have every legal right to kick him out of the house before he gains any right to stay. My head tells me it won't be that easy, though. Jess had to use her police background to warn him off. I have nothing.

The scariest thing was Jess telling me that there isn't anything that *can* be done. With no evidence — or even suspicion — that Tom's broken any laws, the police won't get involved. Jess gave me details for who to call and what to do if Tom refuses to leave or gets violent again. And she's advised me to make sure I record everything.

That's why tomorrow I'm going to go to a specialist shop on the outskirts of London which sells covert recording equipment. It means I'll be able to store a day's worth of recordings on a tiny chip hidden inside a pen, a plug socket or a photo frame. It all sounds ridiculous saying it, but Jess is right: I need to protect myself. If anything happens, or if Tom gets violent, everything will be recorded and can be used against him.

I don't know whether the next few days will allow me to get my head straight and prepare for what's to come, or if it'll make things worse, making my anxiety build and stopping me from sleeping at all.

Either way, I don't have much choice. I have to go home and keep up appearances. For now. There's nowhere else I can go. There's nothing else I can do. And that's why I hope to God the plan works.

When Tom called me last night to tell me he was about to board his flight, I almost had a full-blown anxiety attack. I've managed to keep a lid on things for the past few days. Thankfully he's only been able to call me once a day while he's been away, and I've been able to hold it together for the ten or fifteen minutes we had to speak.

I told him I was having to go through my contents insurance for a replacement phone as I didn't have any money. Partially true. My old phone is off — and staying off — and hidden in the box of Christmas decorations in the loft. That gives me the best part of a year to get rid of it or work out how to transfer things I need off of it and onto a new device without it registering as being switched on.

Even though I knew he was going to be in the air for over eleven hours and wouldn't be home until this morning, I still froze with fear every time I heard a car pass the house or someone making a noise outside. It's crazy. I know I need to calm down. If I'm reacting like this to absolutely nothing, how am I going to be when Tom walks through that door? I need to keep a level head. If he spots any sort of weakness or insecurity, he'll capitalise on it and take control of the situation.

I decide that preparedness is key. I've checked and double-checked the recording gizmos I bought. There are two: both ballpoint pens with hidden microphones, each of which can record up to twenty-four hours of audio. One's on the side in the kitchen, and the other is in the living room. They even function as working pens, which I found both impressive and scary at the same time. I've set them both running already. Tom isn't due to even land for another twenty minutes, but with twenty-four hours of recording space, I can afford to play it safe.

I use my laptop to track his flight, and it eventually lands a little ahead of schedule. Fifteen minutes later, Tom texts me to tell me he's landed and is through passport control. I estimate it'll probably take him a good half an hour to pick up his luggage and get back to his car, plus an hour to drive home. All of a sudden, that doesn't seem very long at all.

The time passes quickly, and I'm only about ten minutes out on my estimate when I hear the sound of Tom's car parking up outside. I look out of the bedroom window and watch as he opens the driver's door, walks round to unlock the boot and takes his suitcase out before walking towards the house.

At that moment, my phone rings. I look at the screen. It's Cath.

'Cath, sorry. Can I call you back?'

'Uh, yeah. But listen. There's something you need to know. It's about Matt.'

I hear the thud of Tom resting his suitcase against the front door while he searches for his keys.

'Cath, please. I've got to go. I'll call you back.'

I hang up the phone, take a deep breath and walk downstairs. I've practiced what I'm going to say over and over in my head over the past few days, like an actor about to walk out on stage.

I hear him fumbling with his key in the lock, trying to figure out why it won't work. It's because I've had the locks changed, Thomas. I've been planning ahead. You might have thought you were the one in charge, but you're not. Not any more.

I wait for him to knock on the door, then I insert my own key and unlock it, before opening the door to the man I've spent the last few months loving, but who now seems like a stranger to me.

'My key doesn't work for some reason,' he says, looking at me.

'I know,' I reply. 'There's a reason for that. I think we need to talk.'

47

Tom steps inside the house with his suitcase, and I have to admit he's doing a great job of looking confused.

'What's this all about?' he asks, putting his case down in the hall. 'What's going on?'

'I've been doing a lot of thinking recently, Tom. I don't think we're right for each other. I think we should go our separate ways.'

He looks at me for a few moments as this registers with him. 'This is about the night of the wedding, isn't it?' he asks.

'What about it?' I say, remembering there are two recording devices that could pick up a confession here.

He ignores my question. 'Did you get the locks changed?'

'They're my locks. I wasn't feeling safe after I had my phone stolen, so I wanted to upgrade my security.'

'You had them changed to keep me out, didn't you?'

'Don't be ridiculous,' I tell him. 'I just let you in, didn't I?'

'Why are you doing this, Grace?'

I avert my eyes to avoid meeting his gaze. 'I just don't think we're best suited to each other. Not after what happened.'

'After *what* happened?'

I look at him. 'After you pinned me to that wall and tried to strangle me the night of Cath's wedding, Tom. What did you think I meant?'

'Are you serious? I've never laid a finger on you in my life! Not on anyone, in fact. Where on earth has all this come from? Are you okay?'

I let out a half-laugh half-snort. 'Don't treat me like an idiot. Are you going to make out I imagined it now?'

'Not imagined it, no. But you were extremely drunk, Grace. Bear in mind I was totally sober that night, so I think I've probably got a better memory of events than you have.'

He's good. But not good enough.

'Oh, my memory is just fine, don't you worry. I don't forget things. I don't have memory lapses. I don't do things and then wipe them from my mind.' As I speak, I can feel myself getting more and more worked up, angrier and angrier at the man who tried to ruin my life and is now standing before me, trying to deny it.

'What on earth are you talking about, Grace? What's going on?'

'I know what you've been doing, Tom,' I tell him, my voice shaking with anger. 'I know who you are.'

His gaze turns less confused, more serious. 'Alright. Go on then. Tell me.'

'You forwarded that email to Matilda, didn't you? The one I sent to Sue.'

'I have no idea what you're talking about.'

'Yes you do. You don't need to tell me, though. I know. Here's something you can tell me, though. How did you find out where my nan lived? How did you get into the house? Why did you take the necklace?'

As he looks at me, his face blank and expressionless, I can see he knows exactly what I'm talking about. He knows. He did it.

'What necklace? Honestly, Grace, I don't know what you're going on about.'

'The one you took from my nan's house and hid in my coffee jar, because you knew that's exactly where my mum and dad would find it when they came over. You knew they were looking for it, you knew they were upset and you wanted to make it look as though I'd stolen it.'

'This is crazy. Why the hell would I want to do that?'

'To push me away from them, and them from me. Because that's what you do, isn't it? You try to isolate women from their family and friends. That's why you told Cath I'd made that Bridezilla comment. It's why you blocked her number on my phone. You knew it'd drive a wedge between us. That's why you forward that work email to Matilda. You knew we'd lose her as a client and I'd potentially lose my job. I'd have become emotionally and financially dependent on you. And that's been your aim all along.'

'Jesus Christ, Grace. Where has this all come from? It's absolute madness. How on earth do you expect me to have broken into a house I didn't know about or forwarded emails from an account I have no access to?'

'That's what I want you to tell me. I want you to admit what you are and what you've been trying to do, and I want you to tell me every detail. I have a right to know.'

Tom lets out a laugh. 'You've got a right to absolutely nothing after accusing me of all that. I've been perfect for you, Grace. I've been everything you wanted, right from the start.'

'Just like you were with all the others?'

Tom's eyes narrow as he studies me. 'What do you mean? What others?'

'Erin. Jess.'

There's a minute flicker in his eyes — barely perceptible, but enough for me to notice — as I say Jess's name.

'I don't know anyone called Jess,' he says.

'Funny. I do.'

He looks at me, willing me to continue. So I do.

'She got in contact with me,' I tell him. 'But then again you already knew that, because you deleted the email thinking I hadn't seen it. But I had. You know, that email account you claim you don't have access to. I went to see her, Tom. Down in Cornwall. She told me everything. Everything you'd done to her, everything you'd done before and since. How you called her your Butterfly. How you tried to isolate her from her family and friends. Pulled her off social media. Tried to ruin her life and make sure she was completely reliant on you. But it didn't work, did it? And it's not going to work with me, either. She found out who you were, and so did I. So I suggest you do exactly the same as you did with her, and walk out. Go somewhere else. Stay out of my life. And take a long, hard look at yourself before you even think about getting involved with other women.'

He shakes his head slowly. 'This is absolutely insane. Grace, I live with you. I love you. You love me. Why the hell would you even believe a word a psychopathic ex-girlfriend tells you over me? There's a reason I left that woman, and it's not because she told me to, I can promise you that.'

'You're lying, Tom.'

'No, I'm not. I promise you, I'm not.'

'There you go again. One lie after another. You can't help yourself, can you? Let me tell you this, Tom. I know all about your lies. All of them. I know who you are. I know what's gone on. And yes, do you know what? I actually feel sorry for you. But maybe now you can accept it and move on like a normal person.'

'Move on from what? What are you talking about?'

'I'm talking about Erin, Tom. She didn't leave you, did she? She didn't take your daughter and do a runner. I know what happened. I know she died, Tom. I know they both died in a car accident — the one you claim your parents died in. But your parents aren't dead, are they? They're alive, Tom. I know they're alive because I found out where they live. Jess told me. I parked up outside their house and watched them, Tom. I sat there for an hour as your dad washed his car and your mum put the bins out.'

'And you accuse *me* of being a psychopath?'

'So I'm right, am I?'

'Grace, I don't know who you think you were watching, but it wasn't my parents. I've told you what happened to them.'

'No you haven't. You told me what happened to Erin. Except you couldn't handle the fact that they'd been taken away from you. You hated the fact your parents were still around and they weren't, so you changed your reality, didn't you? You told yourself it was your parents who'd died, and that Erin and your daughter were still alive. You wanted to give yourself hope. I get it. And I feel sorry for you.'

'You're talking rubbish,' he says, his voice a hoarse whisper, tears forming at the edges of his eyes.

'No I'm not, Tom. You know I'm not. You just can't accept your guilt over their deaths. You feel responsible for it, because you'd got blind drunk at the pub and they were coming to pick you up. Yet again. That's why you don't drink much any more, isn't it? That's why you always want to be the one to drive everywhere. You need to come to terms with it, Tom. For your own good.'

'I don't have anything to come to terms with.'

'Yes you do,' I say, taking a stiff, shiny piece of paper out of my pocket and showing it to him. 'You have to come to terms with this.'

Tom looks at the photo and I can see the reflection of his perfect family in the tears that coat his eyes. Just as I think he's about to finally burst into tears, I notice his jaw clenching and the veins beginning to bulge at the sides of his head before he launches himself at me.

48

This time, I'm quicker. This time, I'm sober. I know what he's about to do. I manage to dodge him and throw him off balance and he crashes into the hall wall, stumbling over his suitcase.

I've thought ahead. I've planned for every eventuality. I've left the door unlocked, and I've got my car key in my pocket, just in case I needed to do this. Just in case I needed to run.

'Get the fuck back here, you fucking bitch!' Tom yells at me as I scramble for the door and open it. 'Don't you fucking dare walk out on me!'

I sprint up the front path, every fibre in my body screaming at me as I hear Tom clambering to his feet and running for the door.

'Grace! Grace!' he calls, putting on a show for the neighbours. The change in his tone inside just a couple of seconds is frightening. Couldn't possibly seem angry in front of them, could he? Got to make out he's the reasonable one, just in case anyone's watching. Ever the actor. Ever the planner. But he hasn't planned this one.

I fumble with my car key as I run, and scrabble to press the button to unlock the car. It takes a couple of attempts before it works, and I see Tom come out of the front door and start running up the path.

I hurry to get the car door open, my hands shaking with adrenaline, my whole body coursing as I climb inside and pull the door shut just as Tom reaches it. I push the lock button, hearing the reassuring sound of the car locking a fraction of a second before Tom starts pulling at the handle and banging on the window.

It's not angry. It's not desperate. It's calm and calculated, almost as if I've stormed off in a huff and he's trying to placate me and make me see sense. But I can see right through it. I know what he's doing. He's putting on a show.

I ignore him as best I can and try to start the engine, the key taking an age to slot into the ignition barrel as I tremble with fear and adrenaline. Finally, eventually, the car starts.

I put it into reverse and back out of my parking space and onto the road, leaving Tom floundering as the car shoots backwards. I don't know where I'm going, but I have to go somewhere. I have to get away from here. Get away from him.

I shift the car into first gear, release the clutch and press my foot down hard on the accelerator.

As the car lurches forward, I notice movement to my side. It's Tom. He's stepped out into the road. And it's too late for me to do anything about it.

I let out a gasp and a small scream as he crashes into the windscreen and bounces off, onto the road behind. I stamp on the brake and come to a shuddering halt, stalling the car in the process.

I open my eyes, panting hard, the beat of my heart deafening in my ears. I look in my mirror and see Tom lying on the tarmac, crumpled. I turn my eyes away from the mirror and onto the road in front of me. I could drive away right now. I could restart the engine and floor it. I'd be out of here in no time. Away from it all. Away from Tom. Safe and sound. But my eyes keep getting drawn back to Tom lying in the road. The Tom I thought I knew and knew I loved. And then people arrive. A man comes out of the house opposite and jogs over to Tom. A lady walking her dog leans over him and pulls her phone out of her pocket.

And that's when I know it's all over.

49

I had no choice. There's no way leaving would have made things better. The police would always find me. It'd be a hit and run. No doubt about it. Mitigating circumstances wouldn't even come into it. Tom would always manage to worm his way out of anything else.

It was clear pretty quickly that Tom was okay. He did an impressive job of trying to look as if he was on his last legs, but there was no way he was badly injured. Not at that speed.

As we waited for the emergency services to arrive, I must have felt every emotion under the sun. Anger at Tom for what he'd done. Panic at what would now happen. Relief at having the opportunity to tell the police everything.

They'll be able to speak to Jess. She's one of their own. I stay silent all the way to the police station, telling myself that over and over. I'll let them book me in, get me a solicitor and then I'll tell them everything. I'll make sure they get hold of Jess and find out what Tom's really like. It won't just be my word against his. Not any more.

I always thought police stations would be a little more accommodating and comfortable than the ones on the TV. If anything, they're worse. This one is cold, drab and depressing.

They've arrested me for attempted murder. Not that it matters in the slightest. While I'm here, I'm safe. I'm in the best possible hands, with people who can help me. All I need to do is make them aware that I'm the victim, not the criminal.

They process me at the custody desk, take my details, ask me if I've drunk any alcohol or taken any drugs recently, then take my shoes and belt off me. As if I'm going to hang myself in my cell. Tempting, but no.

I'm scared. Of course I'm scared. I'm petrified. I've never been arrested in my life. I'd never even set foot inside a police station until Bideford. But now I'm in a cell of my own.

But there's something else that overrides the fear. It's the knowledge that this will soon be over. That I can tell them everything. They're arranging a solicitor for me, and as soon as I get to speak to him I'll hopefully find out if there's something more that can be done. A restraining order, perhaps. Either way, I need to get this all over and done with. I need to move on with my life.

I don't know how long I'm in my cell, but eventually the door opens and a police officer tells me my solicitor is here and wants to speak with me.

I'm taken through into a small room that's more like a stationery cupboard masquerading as a meeting room, and I sit down with the man who introduces himself as Brian Conway. I tell him everything: that Tom deliberately jumped out in front of my car while I was trying to escape from him, that he's a liar and a conman who's been trying to systematically destroy my life and that there's a police officer in Cornwall who can back up absolutely everything I'm saying. He listens intently, but I get the feeling he thinks I'm some sort of mad woman who's trying to dump an insane story on him in an attempt to prove I'm not crazy.

He jots down a few notes, but I don't think he's convinced. He probably hears all sorts of excuses and sob stories, and I doubt very much if this is coming across as the most sensible one. He tells me he recommends giving the police a pre-prepared statement, but I tell him no — I want to tell them everything myself. I don't want to come across as the sort of person who's going to say 'no comment' to everything. I want to cooperate with them, let them see it's actually me who's the victim, not Tom.

A short while after our briefing, we go through to the interview room where two plain-clothes officers introduce themselves as Detective Inspector Jane McKenna and Detective Constable Mark Brennan.

McKenna takes the lead. 'Grace, you've been arrested

for the attempted murder of Thomas Ramsay. Can you explain your relationship to Mr Ramsay please?'

'He's my boyfriend. Ex-boyfriend.'

'Recent ex?'

'Very recent. About thirty seconds before... before what happened.'

'And what did happen?'

I take a deep breath, then let it all out. 'We had an argument in the house. I told him it was over. He launched himself at me and tried to attack me. He's done that before, last week. This time I got out of the way. I decided I had to run, because he's dangerous. So I got into my car and went to drive away, but he threw himself in front of it to make it look as if I'd hit him.'

'Why would he do that?'

'Because he's crazy. He's manipulative.'

'Let's go back to the beginning,' McKenna says. 'We're looking at attempted murder here. Were you driving the car that hit Thomas Ramsay?'

'Yes.'

'Did you drive that car at Thomas Ramsay deliberately?'

'No. I was trying to drive away. He threw himself in front of the car.'

'Did you intend to kill Thomas Ramsay?'

'No.'

'Did you intend to injure or otherwise harm Thomas Ramsay?'

I swallow. 'No.'

The interview turns clinical, as if the officers are only keen to cover the basics. There's no opportunity to tell my side of the story. Barely ten minutes later, the interview is terminated and I'm taken back to my cell.

50

It's a few hours later when they finally take me in for a second interview. They can keep me in for twenty-four hours, apparently. More, if they get authorisation to do so.

When the interview starts, McKenna briefly covers what we spoke about in the first interview, then asks me if I still agree with all of those statements.

'Yes,' I say. 'But I want the opportunity to tell you the background. My side of the story. I want you to know who Tom is, what he's done to me. I'm not the criminal here. I'm the victim. I promise you.'

'That's what this interview is for, Grace,' McKenna says. 'But it's also for us to put some other questions to you based on things we've investigated and discovered in the interim.'

'Okay,' I say, nodding furiously. 'Good.'

'What was the catalyst behind your breakup with Thomas Ramsay, Grace?'

I let out a large sigh. 'Jesus. Well, he's crazy. He's a liar, a psychopath. He's manipulative. He attacked me, last week. He tried to attack me again today when I told him things were over between us.'

'Okay. Do you have any evidence of this?'

'There are recordings,' I say, suddenly remembering the equipment I bought. 'Two pens. There's one on the side in the kitchen, and one in the living room. They've got microphones and things in them. They're set to record. They'll have picked up what happened before I ran outside. The argument. The things we both said. Everything will be on those.'

'You set up covert recording equipment in your own house?' McKenna says, one eyebrow raised.

'Yes. Because of everything he's been doing to me. I've had to. I'm not crazy. I had to do it because of the things he does, because of who he is.'

'Can you tell us any specifics?'

'Yeah. He's tried to break me up with my friends. He stole some jewellery from my nan's house and tried to make out it was me.'

'Jewellery?'

'A necklace.'

'When was this?'

'Uh, about six weeks ago I think.'

'Can you talk us through what happened?'

'My nan died,' I say. 'She'd been ill for a while. She had dementia. There was a necklace she always wore. Amethyst. I always really liked it, and when she died it went missing. My parents blamed me, but I hadn't gone anywhere near it. Tom took it.'

'How do you know he took it?'

'It was in the coffee jar in our kitchen.'

McKenna nods slowly. 'Okay. That doesn't necessarily mean it was him, though, does it?'

'It couldn't have been anyone else.'

'Could you potentially have done it and, I don't know, forgotten about it? Had some sort of memory lapse?'

'No. Definitely not.'

'Have you had memory lapses in the past?'

'No.'

McKenna and Brennan share a look.

'Let's talk about life in general. How about work. Do you work?'

'Sort of. Not at the moment.'

'Oh? Why's that?'

I sigh, and feel Brian squirm beside me. 'I'm suspended.'

'What for?'

'Officially? Gross misconduct. I sent an email to my boss about a client, and apparently sent it to the client as well.'

'An angry email?'

'I guess.'

'Aggressive?'

'I'd say more sarcastic. I'm not an aggressive person. But I don't know how it ended up with the client. I didn't do it. I didn't send it.'

'Does anyone else have access to your emails?'

I think about this for a moment. 'Well, no. But I think Tom hacked in somehow.'

'Hacked in?'

'Yeah. I don't know how it works, but I can't think of any other explanation.'

'Is it possible you could have sent it accidentally? Or perhaps you forgot that you'd done it?'

I narrow my eyes and shake my head. 'No. No, that's not possible.'

'And what about while you're suspended from work, Grace? How are things financially?'

'Well, not great, obviously. Mum and Dad were contributing towards my mortgage, but now they're not.'

'Because of the falling out?'

'No. Well, sort of. It was before then. There was another falling out.'

'And is this necklace valuable, do you know?'

'I've got no idea. I wouldn't have a clue. Are you trying to accuse me of something? Because there's no way in hell I'd ever consider selling that necklace, even if it was mine, and even if it was worth a million pounds. It's worth far more to me than that. Listen, you need to speak to a detective in Cornwall. Her name's Jess Caton. She knows all about Tom. She's investigated him.'

McKenna writes down Jess's name. 'What was he investigated over?'

'Uh, I don't know exactly.'

'So how do you know Jess Caton?'

'She's Tom's ex.'

McKenna and Brennan share a look. It's one I interpret as not being all that encouraging.

'Okay. And how did you come into contact with her?'

'She emailed me. She tracked me down when she found out Tom and I were dating. She wanted to warn me about him and tell me what he's like. He's a pathological liar. He tried to manipulate her too, and he was doing it to me. He attacked me. And when I found out what he was like, I had to run. He's dangerous. You have to believe me.'

McKenna leans back in her chair. 'What do you mean "what he's like"?'

'He lied to me. About everything. He told me his ex — the one before Jess — he told me she'd left him and taken their daughter with her. But she didn't. She died. They both did. There was a car accident.'

McKenna glances at Brennan. 'And was this investigated?'

'Yeah. It was down in Cornwall. Tom was in the pub. They were going to pick him up.'

'So he wasn't involved in any way with the accident itself?'

'Well, no. But he lied about it.'

'Lying isn't illegal, Grace. If he wasn't involved in their deaths that doesn't make him any sort of threat. It's entirely up to him if he wanted to tell you about it or not. Maybe he didn't want to have to explain what had happened.'

'No. I know. But he told me his parents were dead too, but they're not. They're alive. I've seen them.'

'Grace, I'm sorry, but I fail to see what this has to do with anything. I understand you might have been unhappy about all of that, and it's entirely your decision if that's something you wanted to end your relationship over, but I'm not sure it strikes me as justification for running him over.'

'I didn't run him over!' I say, my voice getting louder. 'He threw himself in front of my car!'

Brian puts his hand on my arm and leans in to whisper to me. He tells me it'd be a good idea for me to calm down. I'm angry, upset, but lucid enough to know that he's got a fair point. Showing myself to be an aggressive person isn't the sort of thing that's likely to help cancel out a charge of attempted murder.

'I think it would be best if my client and I took some time out to discuss matters,' Brian says.

51

On Brian's advice, we prepared a statement signed by me, which we gave to McKenna. In it, I repeated my denial of having assaulted Tom or having attempted to harm or injure him in any way, and went into detail about everything Tom had done to me, as well as the things Jess told me he'd done to her. I wanted to make sure they had absolutely everything on record, and that was my condition for agreeing to prepare a statement.

After that, I was taken back to my cell, and I finally managed to get my head down for a while. It can't have been for long, because I wake up feeling worse than I did before. But at least I've got everything out there. I've got it all off my chest. It's officially on police records now. And I just hope and pray they'll get in touch with Jess and corroborate everything.

A short while later, my cell door opens and McKenna's standing in the doorway.

'Grace. Time to go,' she says.

'What do you mean?'

'You're free to go. We're satisfied no crime was committed.'

'What do you mean no crime was committed? Did you listen to the recordings on the pens?'

'No pens were found, Grace. We had officers search your property, but there weren't any recording pens in your kitchen or living room. Only a couple of biros on the kitchen table.'

My face drops. Tom found them. He got there first, and got rid of them.

'So you don't believe me?'

McKenna steps into the cell and sits down on the hard "bed" next to me. 'We do, as it happens. We take these sorts of things extremely seriously. We've got officers on patrol looking for Tom as we speak.'

'What do you mean looking for him? He went to hospital, didn't he?'

McKenna shuffles awkwardly. 'He did, and he was discharged as he didn't have any injuries requiring treatment.'

'So why wasn't he arrested at that point?'

'Because he'd been discharged before we spoke to you about the abuse, Grace. I know. I'm disappointed too. But all we can do now is find Tom, arrest him and put your allegations to him.'

'Can I stay here until you find him?'

'I wish it was that simple. I'd struggle to justify keeping you in a cell when you've been cleared of any crime at the best of times, but we've just had word that we've got a bunch of football hooligans being brought in after a brawl outside the cup match tonight. Is there somewhere safe you can go?'

I run through a few options in my mind. I can't go home, because Tom could be there. He knows where my parents live, so that's not an option either. 'I could go to my friend's place,' I say. 'Cath Baker. There'll be three of us then, and she lives in a flat so he wouldn't even be able to get as far as her front door. She only lives the other side of Tesco's. I could be there in less than two minutes.'

'Okay. We'll need to take a note of the address so we know where you are. Would you like someone to escort you there?'

I think about this for a moment before answering. 'Does Tom know I'm here?'

'No. He knows you were arrested, but he doesn't know which station you're in or that you're being released. No-one's been able to get hold of him for hours.'

That's when it all makes sense. He's done a runner. The second the police get close, he's gone. He did exactly the same when Jess told him she knew what he was — who he was.

'It'll be fine,' I say. 'You've got enough to be dealing with. I've only got to walk through a supermarket car park.'

Once I've left my cell, I'm formally told I'm being released without charge and my personal belongings are given back to me.

The police let me call Cath, and I tell her what's happened and ask if I can come to hers. She tells me Ben's out at the pub with a friend but will be back in an hour or so, and she's looking after Ben's niece and nephew, so she can't leave them while they're asleep. I tell her it's fine — I'll only be a few minutes.

'Your phone,' McKenna asks me. 'Is that the new one you bought?'

'Yeah. He can't track it.'

'Alright. Keep it on anyway, okay? Call me on this number as soon as you get to Cath's flat and are inside.' She hands me a business card.

'I will,' I say. 'And thanks.'

They let me out the back way into the police car park, then unlock a gate so I can take the most direct route — through Tesco's car park and over the crossing to Cath's flat. First, though, there's something I need to do.

I go into Tesco's and head straight to the wine aisle. I pick up two bottles of Pinot Grigio, head to the checkout and pay for them. As I'm halfway across the car park, my phone rings. I answer it.

'Grace, it's Jane McKenna.'

'Oh, hi. I'm not quite there yet. I popped into Tesco's to

get some wine. Figured we could do with it after the day I've had.'

'Grace, stay on the phone for me until you get there, alright? We're going to walk an officer over to you to make sure you're okay.'

'Why? What's wrong?' I ask. There's a tone to McKenna's voice which makes me feel uneasy.

'We've just had a call from Devon and Cornwall Police,' she says.

I feel the blood draining from my face.

'Why? What's the problem? Oh god. She wasn't actually a police officer, was she?'

'Yes. Yes, she was,' McKenna replies.

'So what's the problem? Why can't you speak to her?'

'Because she's dead, Grace.'

52

I freeze on the spot.

'What?' I say, my voice almost a whisper.

'We don't know what's happened yet, but we want to make sure you're safe. We're sending an officer over to make sure you get to Cath's without any issues.'

I understand straight away what this means. My life is in immediate danger. Tom has killed Jess Caton, and I'm next.

As I'm about to speak again, a figure emerges from behind a parking ticket machine. I recognise it immediately. It's Tom.

UNTITLED

You have no idea how good it feels to see you again. I've waited so long. Traveled so far. Gone through so much. I always knew you'd come back to me.

You look so delicate, so fragile and elegant. My butterfly. I gave you those wings. I held you inside that chrysalis, that protective cocoon, to stop you from feeding on that poison. And now look at what you've become. I was so proud of you. Was.

I created you. I thought I was doing the right thing. So did Dr Frankenstein. Did you know that was actually the doctor's name, and not the monster? But these days everyone thinks Frankenstein was the monster, not the doctor. Isn't it strange how people can get so muddled up as to which one is the real monster?

Of course, the doctor and the monster both die. The doctor dies first, running away from the monster he created.

But not before he agrees to go back home and face his creation.

The only person who could have cared for the monster was the good doctor. He was the only one who understood him, who knew what made him tick. I must say, I sympathise entirely. And now we face our own final chapter.

53

I can't speak.

Tom takes my phone and ends the call.

'In the car. Now,' he says, showing me a large knife.

I could run, but he'd catch me immediately. I look behind me, but there's no sign of the police officer McKenna told me they'd sent. Before I have a chance to decide what to do next, Tom grabs hold of me, opens the car door and shoves me inside. Within a couple of seconds he's in the driver's seat, has started the engine and we're on the move.

He pulls out onto the main road and quickly builds up speed, steering with one hand as he switches my phone off with the other and puts it in his jacket pocket.

'Where are we going?' I ask.

'Just for a little chat.'

'I don't want to chat. I want to go home. I want to be on my own.'

'You will be.'

Tom drives out of town and out onto a rural lane. I've been down here once or twice before, but it's not an area I know well. As we get further and further out, there are fewer and fewer cars, until Tom pulls over into a small car park by some woodland.

'Wait there,' he says. 'I'll come round and let you out.'

'Where are we going?' I ask when he opens the door. 'I don't want to get out.'

'Do as you're told.'

'What are you going to do?'

He ignores me. I get out of the car, swallow, then try to force out the words I've been wanting to ask. 'What happened to Jess?'

'You know what happened to Jess. She's gone.'

The coldness of his words alongside the chill winter air sends an icy blast right through me, and I shove my hands in my cardigan pockets.

'Did you kill her?' I ask.

I feel something sharp press into the small of my back, and I know in an instant it's a knife.

'Walk.'

'Tom. Please. Don't do this. Just leave. Start a new life somewhere. I won't tell anyone. I promise. Just don't do this. Please.'

He doesn't answer me, but instead presses the knife harder against me until I start to walk, deeper and deeper into the woods.

54

We reach a small clearing and Tom gestures for me to sit down on the trunk of a fallen tree. It's damp and falling to pieces, but I'm in no position to question seating arrangements right now.

We sit in silence for a couple of minutes before Tom speaks.

'Why did you have to do it, Grace? Why did you have to go and visit that fucking bitch?'

'She contacted me. She told me things. I wanted to find out the truth.'

'I don't know what this obsession is with the truth. Why do things have to be "true"? Sometimes the truth isn't the most convenient thing, you know. Sometimes there are very good reasons for things not being true. Sometimes it's a hell of a lot easier if they aren't.'

'But you can't hide from what happened, Tom,' I say,

almost pleading. 'I know what happened to Erin. It wasn't your fault. It was an accident. It's not healthy for you to not come to terms with that. You need to be able to accept what happened.'

'Accept it? *Accept* it?'

'You know what I mean. It wasn't your fault, Tom.'

For the first time, I see a tear running from his eye.

'Yes it was. It was my choice to go out drinking and leave them on their own. It was my choice to demand they came to pick me up. I could have got a taxi. But I didn't.'

'There's no way you could have known what was going to happen. For all you knew, you could've got a taxi, they stayed at home and the house could've caught fire. You can't take responsibility for that.'

'That's not the sort of thing you can dictate,' he says quietly. 'I thought you were what I needed. You reminded me of her.'

'I know,' I say, thinking back to how similar Jess and I looked, and how she told me Erin had looked the same too.

'I didn't want to kill her,' he says, almost as if he's followed my exact train of thought. 'She left me no choice. I had to protect myself. I had to protect the memory of Erin. She wanted to destroy that. She wanted to destroy us. I lost Erin, then thought I had it back with Jess. When I found you, I had it all again. Until she popped back up and tried to ruin it.' There's an anger in Tom's voice that's almost visceral. 'I've been through too much. I've lost too much. And every single time I've had to build it back up from scratch. I can't risk that happening again.'

'It doesn't have to be that way, Tom.'

He shakes his head. 'It does. We both know it does. We know the way this ends. I don't want it to have to be like that, but it does. We've got no choice now. I don't want to have to do this, but I can't face you leaving me alone again, like she did. Like they both did. I can't have that being my fault again.'

I think I can see a way in. I think I might be able to talk him round. If only to save my own life.

'None of it was your fault, Tom. Erin's death wasn't your fault. Jess leaving you was her choice. You weren't compatible. She didn't know you. Not like I know you.'

'You're the only one who has,' he says, his voice hoarse. 'You're the only one who knows the truth now.'

'I know. And that means so much to me, Tom.'

'You must think I'm crazy,' Tom says, running his finger along the blade of the knife, the metal glinting occasionally as it catches the light of the moon.

'No, not at all,' I say. 'Don't forget I know you. I understand you.'

'Where did you get the photo from?' he asks, his voice calm and quiet.

'Jess gave it to me. I don't know where she got it.'

Tom nods slowly.

'Tom, will you tell me everything? About Jess. Erin. The necklace. The email.'

'Why? What's the point?'

'Because we're being open and honest now. You can tell me everything, and I can tell you everything.'

'You don't need to tell me anything,' Tom says.

'I know. But I want to.'

'No, I mean you don't need to. I already know. You drove down to Bodmin to find Jess, but you stopped at Bideford for a bit first. And Chieveley Services on the way.'

I don't know how he knows this, but I see absolutely no point in denying it. That'll only rile him.

'Yeah. Yeah I did. I mis-remembered the email and thought she'd said Bideford. It was gone when I woke up. How did you manage to get in and delete it?'

'I work in online security, Grace,' he replies, a deadpan on his face. 'It's our job to stop people getting in. To stop someone doing something, the first thing you need to know is how they're going to do it.'

'You put a tracker on my car, didn't you?'

'Easily done. Ten minutes on eBay, that one.'

'Did you think I hadn't seen the email?'

'Honestly?' he says, looking at me. I nod. 'Yeah. Yeah, I thought I'd got there before you. You were absolutely steaming and I assumed you'd just crash out. It was showing as unread when I saw it. I called you when I landed and you seemed fine. A bit hungover and pissed off, but you definitely didn't sound like you'd read that email.'

My acting skills haven't faded too much over the years, then.

'When did you realise I'd seen it?' I ask.

'I checked the tracker after we spoke on the phone. That's when I saw you'd gone to Cornwall.'

'And what did you do?'

Tom stays silent for a few moments, and I don't push him for an answer.

'I explained I had a family emergency back home and booked onto the next available flight.'

My breath catches as I hear Tom say this. I know where it's leading. 'You were in the UK?'

'Only a day or so before I was meant to be coming back anyway. By then I knew you were home again.'

'So you went to Cornwall?'

Tom nods.

'Did you kill Jess because she knew the truth? Because she told me?'

Tom stands up. 'I think we should go now.'

'Tom, please. I want to know. I need to know. If we're going to be together, we both have to be completely open and honest with each other.'

He looks at me, his eyes almost like a puppy's. In that moment I see something vulnerable, lost.

'Please, Tom. Let's do this properly. You and me.'

He sits back down on the log, slowly. He's silent for a while, before he starts to talk.

'I'm not a bad person, Grace. I don't do things to people just because they've upset me. It's not about that. Jess ruined my life twice. I adored her. I lost her. I had to leave my home town. My friends. And then I found you.'

I put my hand on top of his, trying desperately to ensure I'm not shaking with nerves.

'I'd let it go, you see. Jess. Time to start afresh. When I saw your profile, I couldn't breathe. I knew I'd found you. And when I saw the picture of you in the butterfly dress, it suddenly all made sense. It was almost too good to be true. You were perfect. My butterfly. Delicate. Beautiful.'

'Like Erin?'

Tom nods. 'And then she tried to ruin that for me, too. That's when I knew she was never going to back down. She was never going to give up. I knew she'd probably ended us, and if I ever found happiness again she'd end that too. She had to go. I had no choice.'

'I understand,' I say, fighting every cell of my body urging me to run. 'But you haven't lost me. I'm still here.'

'You didn't want to be here. I saw the look in your eyes.'

'I was scared, Tom. This is all new to me. I didn't know your reasons. All I knew is you hurt me, told me things that weren't true and then killed Jess. And yes, I thought you were crazy. Insane. But I didn't know the truth, did I? I didn't know you were only doing it to protect me. To protect us.'

Tom looks at me, and I give him the most loving, understanding look I can muster in that moment.

'Do you really mean it?' he asks.

'Yes,' I say. 'Yes, I do.'

He leans over and kisses me, gently at first, as if testing the water. I respond, closing my eyes and putting myself in different shoes, with a different person. A short while later, he puts his forehead against mine and looks into my eyes, before pulling me into a tight embrace.

'I love you,' he says.

'I love you too.'

'Do you?' he asks.

'Yes. Absolutely.'

Tom lets out a huge breath and his body seems to relax, losing all its pent-up tension. He puts his head in his hands and seems to cry.

I kneel down in the dirt and stones, trying to show some concern.

'I thought I'd lost you,' he says. 'I really thought I'd lost you.'

I stroke his hair and pull him in towards me, ensuring we don't make eye contact. Then I lift the rock from the ground and swing it through the air, bringing it crashing down on the back of his skull.

55

Tom crumples to the ground with the slightest of grunts, and his head hits the floor with a sickening thud. I'd planned to hit him and run, but then again I was expecting him only to be injured and set back a few seconds. I wasn't expecting him to be completely unconscious, bleeding profusely onto the dirt.

In the silence of the night, I hear the slightest of gurgles escaping his lips and I decide I need to run. Need to call the police. I shove my hand into his jacket pocket and grab my phone. Then I turn on my heels as suddenly as I can, and dart off back in the direction we came from.

I run as fast as my legs can carry me, the bones and joints searing with pain as the sudden strenuous exercise fights against my freezing cold legs. The muscles feel fit to burst, but I push through. I have to. I need to.

As I run, I fumble in my coat pocket for my mobile

phone. It's still switched off from when Tom grabbed me in the car park, and I force my frozen fingers to hold the right buttons to turn it on.

I glance behind me, just to check I'm not being followed, and wait an eternity for my phone to spring to life. When it finally does, I look in the corner of the screen. There's no signal.

Shit.

I slow down, moving in one direction, desperately willing my phone to pick up a signal from somewhere. I'm focused completely on the screen, clenching my jaw as I wait for one — just one — tiny little bar to appear to let me know I can make a call.

I don't know how long I move around for, or in which direction, but when that signal finally appears I'm overjoyed.

I tap in 999 and press *Call*. The call connects almost instantly.

'Emergency services, which service do you require?'

'Police. Quickly.'

'Please hold. Connecting you.'

The next couple of seconds are the longest in my life.

'Hello, where are you calling from?' says a new voice.

'Uh, I don't know. I'm in the middle of some woods. It's down a lane outside of town. I don't know where I am. My ex has kidnapped me and brought me out here. He's got a knife. He's trying to kill me. I managed to hit him with a rock and I've run away, but I don't know where I am or where he is.'

'Okay, we're going to try and locate your call. Can you see any distinctive features around you?'

'Trees. Just trees.'

'Alright. Are you injured?'

'No.'

'And you mentioned there was a weapon involved, is that right?'

'Yes, he's got a knife.'

'Okay. We've located your call and officers are on their way. What's your name?'

I want to answer. I want to tell him my name. But I can't. Because I've got sight of the clearing where Tom and I sat on the log a few minutes ago. I can see the log. I can see the rock. I can see the pool of blood. But I can't see Tom.

56

I'm frozen to the spot. I have no idea where Tom is. There's no sign of him. No sound. Nothing.

Has he run away? I didn't hear him get up, didn't have any indication he went in the same direction as me. If he was conscious enough to have got up a few seconds later, he must have been conscious enough to have noticed which direction I'd run in. He must have escaped. At the very least, that means he's not after me. I hope.

But something tells me I shouldn't be so sure. Tom's clever. Manipulative. This is just his sort of game. Just the sort of thing he thrives on. If he can see me, scared out of my mind, panicking, he'll be in his element.

He'll want me dead. I know he will. But if he knows I've called the police there's a greater chance he'll have fled. He disappeared when Jess threatened him with her position, and he's in even deeper shit now. There's no way he'll have risked sticking around, is there?

I can't take any chances. I spot an opening in some bushes and I quietly manoeuvre myself inside them.

'My name's Grace,' I whisper gently into the phone. 'Grace O'Sullivan. My ex is Tom Ramsay. DI Jane McKenna knows everything. Please hurry, please.'

There's no response from the other end of the phone. I take it away from my ear and look at the screen. Fuck. The signal's gone again.

I squeeze my eyes shut and pull myself into a ball, praying to whatever god exists that they've taken me seriously, that the police are on their way.

I don't know how long I sit there — time is the first of my senses to have disappeared — but after a short while the interminable silence and darkness is broken by a distant movement of light.

It takes me a few moments to work out what it is, but then it dawns on me. Flashing blue lights. The police. They're here.

I move onto my knees and shuffle out of the bush as quietly as I can, my ankles frozen solid as I rise to my feet and make a run in the direction of the lights. If I can reach the police, I'll be safe.

Every bone in my legs feels like it's about to snap, my muscles tight with the freezing cold, but I'm running, heading for the flashing blue lights. Heading for freedom.

Until, out of the darkness of the night, steps Tom.

The first thing I feel is a dull sensation in my abdomen.

My body crumples, unable to take the weight, and I land on my back in the wet leaves with a thud.

The dull sensation in my abdomen becomes a fierce, fiery pain.

The warm blood trickles around my sides, tickling them, as it pools around my back.

I hear other noises. Shouting. Angry voices.

Get down on the floor! Drop the knife!

Tom's eyes meet mine as mine meet darkness.

The bright light burns my eyes and I squint and fight against opening them, but there's just enough detail coming through to know I'm not at home in my bed.

My throat feels swollen. No, not swollen. Odd. Like I can't swallow. Like there's something there. My stomach feels like it's been torn open. My legs are tight and fiery. The thirst is unreal. I need water.

Bright lights.

'Grace?'

A voice. One I recognise. It's my dad.

'I'll fetch the nurse.'

Mum.

I fade back out again, back to replaying memories of childhood, stretched out on the living room floor, playing with Lego. It feels like I'm there for an age. An entire childhood. But then I'm yanked back to the bright lights.

'You're alright, Grace.' I don't know this voice. It's male. Youngish. American. 'Grace, you're at the General. There's no need to be alarmed, because you're doing great.' Not American. Canadian. 'We're just going to run a few tests on you, okay? Try not to move for us. You've just had a major operation, which went really well, but we need to check a few things now that you're awake.'

I try to nod, but can't. Groan, but that's not happening either.

The nurse runs his tests, pokes and prods me, then removes the tube from my throat. The first time I swallow, it feels as if my oesophagus has stuck together, and I desperately sip at the water they've given me, slurping at the straw like a woman possessed.

The nurse leaves the room, leaving me with Mum and Dad.

'How do you feel?' Mum asks me.

I can't answer that question in fewer than five thousand words, so I settle for 'Shit'.

'We're just so glad you made it through,' she says. 'There were moments when they thought you wouldn't. You lost a lot of blood.'

'Five pints,' Dad says. 'Hope they don't charge you for it. That'd set you back twenty quid at the Fox and Badger.'

I hear the distinctive sound of Mum slapping Dad's wrist.

'What do you remember?' she asks me.

'Not a lot. Tom. Running. Falling.'

'Little shit stabbed you,' Dad says. 'In the belly. He was trying to finish you off when the coppers turned up. Bloody good job they did, too. You'd be brown bread otherwise.'

'I think that's his way of saying he loves you,' Mum adds.

'Okay to come in?' another voice says. McKenna.

She walks over and sits down on a spare chair beside my bed.

'How you feeling?' she asks.

'Shit.'

'You look it. The doctors say you're lucid, so I thought it'd be best if I popped in to update you on what's happened. Tom's been arrested for your attempted murder plus the murder of Jessica Caton. We've not gone to the Crown Prosecution Service yet, but we're hopeful they'll agree to authorise both charges.'

'Hopeful?' Dad asks. 'That doesn't sound promising.'

'It's all we can say at this stage. We've got officers gathering physical evidence as we speak. The more we have before we go to the CPS, the better.'

'But he tried to kill me. And he admitted to killing Jess,' I say, forcing my words out through a hoarse whisper.

'I know. But the CPS's job is to make sure the case is pretty much watertight before it gets to court. Their remit is to make sure public money isn't wasted on trials that won't go anywhere. We need to make sure we've got all our ducks in a row so we don't come a cropper in court.'

'So there's a chance he might get away with it?' Dad asks. I can hear the anger rising in his voice.

'Well, I wouldn't say that. He was standing over Grace, holding the knife that had just been used to stab her, and was trying to attack her again when officers arrived. I'm not saying there's not enough evidence. I'm quite sure there'll be plenty. I'm just keeping you abreast of the procedure and where we are at this present moment. But there's something else you should know.' McKenna's words are met with silence and held breath. It doesn't sound like she's about to deliver good news. 'He's requested a psych eval. A psychiatric evaluation.'

'What does that mean?' Mum asks.

'It means he's requested — or his solicitor has, anyway — for him to be evaluated by a mental health professional.'

Dad makes a snorting noise. 'So he can get away with it and spend a few years in a cosy hospital instead of rotting in a prison cell where he belongs?'

'That's one way of looking at it. Of course, I couldn't possibly comment. That's for the professionals to decide. My job is to make sure we've gathered as much evidence as we can and that we achieve a successful prosecution. For what it's worth, I don't think diminished responsibility on the grounds of mental ill health goes hand in hand with that.'

'He clearly needs help,' Mum says.

'Well, yes. The point we'd like to get to is a sentence that reflects the severity of what he's done and the lives he's ruined, with access to psychiatric support in prison. The two don't have to be mutually exclusive, and we'll be pushing for that option. He's clearly more than capable of operating as a human being and coming across as perfectly normal. He's extremely high functioning.'

'He's insane,' Dad murmurs.

'Not the sort of thing we want to be saying out loud, if I'm honest. Especially if we're pushing for him to be declared psychologically sound. Grace, your friend's been waiting outside most of the night. Cath Baker? Do you want me to let her in?'

I nod, slowly, the joints in my neck creaking as I do so.

McKenna stands up and walks towards the door. A few moments later, Cath comes in.

'Hey you,' she says. 'How are you feeling?'

'Shit.'

'You want to try sitting on a plastic chair all night surviving on nothing but cheap vending machine coffee and Twixes. We've been waiting outside since your mum called last night.'

I didn't realise she'd brought Ben with her. I turn my head towards her. There's no-one else there. Just Cath.

'We?' I ask.

'Yeah. There's someone here who wants to see you.'

'Who?'

There's a noise at the door. I look over to see someone step inside the room.

It's Matt.

'The wanderer returns,' Dad mutters under his breath, the anger and disdain clear in his voice. 'Finished pissing about in Outer Mongolia and thought you'd pony trek your way back into her life, did you?'

'Derek, come on,' Mum says. 'Let's leave them to it, eh?'

Dad looks at her, then at me, grumbling as he does as he's told and rises to his feet. 'Alright. Fine. You can tell her about your chakras and entertain her with your tales of putting lederhosen on a monk in Peru, but then you can bugger off. I'm hungry now. I want a Twix.'

McKenna and Cath follow them, leaving Matt and I alone in the room. I don't know what I'm meant to say to him. I'm marginally more pleased to see him than I would have been to see Tom, but there's not much in it.

'Cath told me everything,' he tells me, sitting down on the chair beside my bed.

'I doubt it. Cath doesn't know everything.'

'She's Cath. She's worked out more than you think.'

'Shame she didn't tell me that a little earlier then.'

'Look, I know you're probably not best pleased to see me. I'm not stupid. I know I hurt you. And your family. Cath almost kicked my head in. And I know you're not going to just let me waltz back into your life as and when I please. I'm not expecting that. But I do want to be able to give you my side of the story. If only to make peace with it myself.'

I raise my eyebrows. How gentlemanly of him to want to satisfy his own guilty conscience.

'How long have you been back?' I ask.

'I got back yesterday. Terrible timing, I know. Never was my strongest suit. Listen, Grace. I didn't want to hurt you. We'd been together since we were kids, Grace. Neither of us ever got the chance to be ourselves. We were a unit. A couple. Neither of us was ever a person in our own right. Not properly. I know that might not have been something you wanted, but I had itches to scratch. Things I needed to do. I never wanted that to be at the expense of our relationship, I promise. But at the same time I knew you had no interest in doing those things with me. You're a homebird. And that's fine. But it was always going to drive us apart. We were always going to want different things. Things that weren't compatible. If there was never going to be any movement or compromise, we were always going to be blown apart.'

I can see where he's coming from, but it does sound a little like he's blaming my immovability for him leaving me. He's right. We probably weren't compatible. Not when it came to our views on life and what we both wanted from it.

'And did you scratch your itch?'

Matt shrugs. 'I guess. To an extent, anyway. I'm always going to be someone who wants to see the world and experience different things. That's never going to change. I'm still going to want to do it. I'm still going to do it. But there's a lot of room in me now for the alternative, too.'

'How do you mean?'

'I dunno. Putting down roots here. Having a home. A conventional life. One that allows me to slip out of convention every now and again when the itch arises. It taught me that the two don't need to be mutually exclusive. They can work together perfectly well if the communication's there. And if everyone involved is on the same page. I saw a lot of the world, Grace. I met a lot of people. I think I'd already started to realise a lot of things long before, but last week I got chatting to a guy over a couple of beers and some sushi. We both opened up about stuff, realised we had a lot in common. He said something about never giving up on what you want. He'd had a rough time of things and had had things taken away from him. So he learned never to take anything for granted. He was only out there for a few days for work, but he said when he got home he had some unfinished business to take care of, and he didn't know which way it was going to go. The main thing was he knew he'd soon find out. And then he'd be at peace. He said I should make my own personal peace, too. That's when I knew I had to come back.'

I lie still in my bed, an icy chill having run down my spine. My blood has run cold. Even though I'm certain I know the answer, I ask the question anyway.

'Where was this?' I ask.

Matt cocks his head slightly and answers. 'Japan. Why?'

59

Sometimes things seem right when they aren't. Sometimes they are. The same could be said of wrong, I suppose. And anyway, who's to say what's right or wrong?

We all need events in our lives to put things into perspective. To see what we really stand to lose or gain. Life's not about achieving perfection: it's about achieving balance. Spend too long reaching for the goals of others and you'll miss your own without ever knowing what they were.

Nothing is perfect. Perfection is unattainable. Even the world's smoothest surface will look like sandpaper under a microscope. And do you know what makes it feel smooth when it isn't? Our hands. The way we detect and interpret the surface. The ridges and imperfections in our own surface, working perfectly in tandem with what we receive.

If any of us ever thinks our life is perfect, or that we ourselves are perfect, we should know that this is our imperfection. True joy is not found in enjoying the comfort and ease of a tranquil life. It's found in seeing the darkness and realising how much light there is in everything else.

Matt's not perfect. Nor am I. Then again, I wouldn't want him to be. I spent too long searching for perfection, only to find it comes wrapped in false platitudes. Ones which nearly cost me my life. No-one needs to be perfect. And no-one needs other people to be happy. The traditional boy-meets-girl doesn't always work.

Life isn't a fairytale, nor should it ever be one. Not in the conventional sense, anyway. Fairytales aren't perfect. Most of them consist of fighting against death and evil, coming through the other side battle-scarred and weary, and with both considerable personal loss and spiritual gain.

If that's the case, let this be my fairytale.

We're friends. We'll see what's there. Neither of us is in any rush. Not anymore. In any case, I've come to realise that I don't need anything more than that. Sure, it's nice to have, but it's not what defines my happiness. It's something that was always there, and which I always thought I needed, but I was wrong. I can be happy.

My suitcase clatters along the uneven paving as we walk towards the terminal, and I look forward to the adventure that awaits me. We won't be gone long. A month or so. We'll play it by ear.

I gave it another fortnight for work to get back to me with a conclusion. They didn't, so I told them to shove it. The last thing I needed was the uncertainty, and it soon became apparent I had more important things to worry about.

Dad doesn't seem best pleased, but he's clearly more

comfortable than he lets on. He and Mum have given us the money to go — an advance on Nan's inheritance. Even he can see that sometimes it's better to just live and let live.

It might sound strange, but I've barely thought about what went on before. What good could it possibly do me? There are reminders, of course, but I try to push them out of my mind and focus on the future. That's the only way anyone is going to be able to move forward. And we all need to move forward.

The police were successful in charging Tom on both counts. He's on remand, awaiting a court date. DI McKenna thinks I'll have to give evidence, and in a strange way I'm looking forward to it. I could worry and panic and focus on the negatives. I could concern myself with having to come face to face with him again, having to be in the same room as him. But I'm not. What good would it do me? I'm framing it as my opportunity to ensure justice is done.

McKenna called round to see me after I got out of hospital. She brought flowers and chocolates. She told me about a case she'd worked on three or so years ago, where a woman was being stalked and made out to be mentally unstable. No-one believed her. And it almost ended in tragedy. She recognised the similarities in me, she said. I'm thankful for that. If that poor woman hadn't gone through her own ordeal, there's every chance I wouldn't be here now.

Matt's told me a lot about Japan. It's another world from here. A completely different model of society. But it's one I want to see. Something I want to experience for myself, if only to say I have. Because what's the alternative? Keep plodding on, doing the same old thing time and time again, living in the same old rut? I've got a chance, an opportunity to do something different. If only for a short while.

We lift our cases onto the check-in conveyer, knowing the next time we see them we'll be in Japan. The land of the rising sun.

I've always wanted to see the cherry blossom. The Japanese believe it symbolises the brevity and cyclical nature of life. Sometimes it's only out for a few days, if that. If there are fierce winds, the delicate blossom is gone in half the time, leaving bare twigs until that season's leaves begin to sprout. As a result, the Japanese associate it with mortality and the acceptance of karma and destiny. They seem somehow symbolic for me now.

If nothing else, it'll be an experience.

ACKNOWLEDGMENTS

It always feels somewhat disingenuous for my name to be writ large on the front cover when the truth is that there's a huge team behind every book.

To begin with, an author must translate the nucleus of an idea into a set of structured beats. When it comes to my books, it's more a case of turning my brain farts into something usable. For that, my thanks go to Mark Boutros for his patience and good humour in being a world-class sounding board for plot and character. He's also unfortunate enough to share my sense of humour and penchant for rubbish football teams.

That does, however, mean that my wife, Joanne, comes second (careful, now). Her continual suggestions for improvements and her unswerving dedication to ensuring each book is as good as it possibly can be is always hugely appreciated. My books would be undoubtedly poorer without her suggestions.

If there are still improvements to be made, these are unfailingly spotted by my mum or my Editor in Chief, Lucy. Lucy has read and edited each of my books over the past ten years, and nobody knows them as well as she does — not even me. She's always the first to tell me if something isn't good enough. And she's always right.

The gorgeous cover is, once again, down to Stuart Bache. Not only is he one of the world's greatest living cover designers, but he's also a good friend.

My biggest thanks, though, must go to the tens of thousands of you who are members of the VIP Club, as well as the 2,000+ in the Adam Croft Readers Group on Facebook. Your daily love is the greatest thing a writer could ask for.

MORE BOOKS BY ADAM CROFT

RUTLAND CRIME SERIES

1. What Lies Beneath
2. On Borrowed Time
3. In Cold Blood

KNIGHT & CULVERHOUSE CRIME THRILLERS

1. Too Close for Comfort
2. Guilty as Sin
3. Jack Be Nimble
4. Rough Justice
5. In Too Deep
6. In The Name of the Father
7. With A Vengeance
8. Dead & Buried
9. In Too Deep
10. Snakes & Ladders

PSYCHOLOGICAL THRILLERS

- Her Last Tomorrow

- Only The Truth
- In Her Image
- Tell Me I'm Wrong
- The Perfect Lie
- Closer To You

KEMPSTON HARDWICK MYSTERIES

1. Exit Stage Left
2. The Westerlea House Mystery
3. Death Under the Sun
4. The Thirteenth Room
5. The Wrong Man

All titles are available to order from all good book shops.

Signed and personalised books available at adamcroft.net/shop

EBOOK-ONLY SHORT STORIES

- Gone
- The Harder They Fall
- Love You To Death
- The Defender

To find out more, visit adamcroft.net

GET MORE OF MY BOOKS FREE!

Thank you for reading *Closer To You*. I hope it was as much fun for you as it was for me writing it.

To say thank you, I'd like to give you some of my books and short stories for FREE. Read on to get yours...

If you enjoyed the book, please do leave a review online. Reviews mean an awful lot to writers and they help us to find new readers more than almost anything else. It would be very much appreciated.

I love hearing from my readers, too, so please do feel free to get in touch with me. You can contact me via my website, on Twitter @adamcroft and you can join my Facebook Readers Group at http://www.facebook.com/groups/adamcroft.

Last of all, but certainly not least, I'd like to let you know that members of my email club have access to FREE, exclusive books and short

stories which aren't available anywhere else. There's a whole lot more, too, so please join the club (for free!) at https://www. adamcroft.net/vip-club

For more information, visit my website: adam-croft.net